SWIMMING
with the WHALES

Ella Thorp Ellis

SWIMMING
with the
WHALES

HENRY HOLT AND COMPANY

NEW YORK

Henry Holt and Company, Inc.
Publishers since 1866
115 West 18th Street
New York, New York 10011

Henry Holt is a registered
trademark of Henry Holt and Company, Inc.

Published in Canada by Fitzhenry & Whiteside Ltd.,
195 Allstate Parkway, Markham, Ontario L3R 4T8.

Library of Congress Cataloging-in-Publication Data
Ellis, Ella Thorp.
Swimming with the whales / Ella Thorp Ellis.
p.   cm.
Summary: When it is proposed that he attend school in the United
States, a fourteen-year-old boy struggles with his parents'
dissolving marriage and his desire to remain near the whales
that annually migrate to the waters near his Patagonian home.
[1. Divorce—Fiction.   2. Fathers and sons—Fiction.
3. Whales—Fiction.   4. Patagonia—Fiction.]   I. Title.
PZ7.E4714Sw   1995   [Fic]—dc20   94-43895

ISBN 0-8050-3306-8

First Edition—1995

Printed in the United States of America
on acid-free paper.∞

10   9   8   7   6   5   4   3   2   1

To Kirk,
who also loves whales

Acknowledgments

Many thanks to the naturalists and their families who contributed to this story so evocatively: Natalie Goodall, Guillermo Harris, Claudio Campagna, and Juan Carlos Lopez, who once swam with killer whales to prove their friendliness to man. A special thank you to the children and teachers of Escuela 87 in Puerto Piramides.

CONTENTS

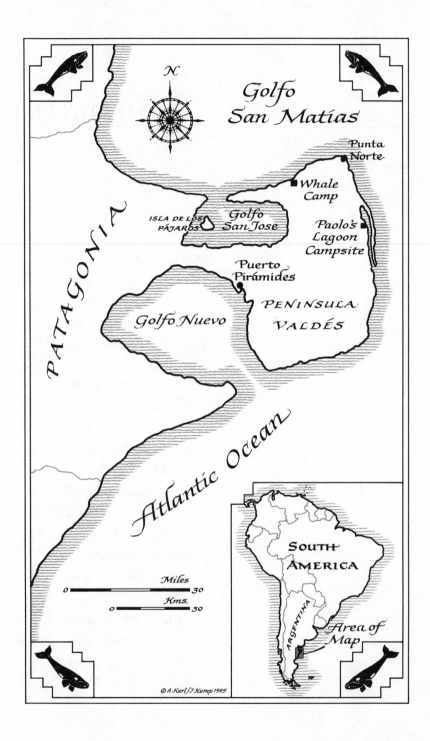

SWIMMING
with the WHALES

WHALES IN THE MORNING

1 The sand felt warm between Paolo's toes, and the bay was so clear he could see perch skimming the sandy bottom. Farther out, the frothy whale blows showed the whales had returned. He had seen the whales diving and felt the rush of water all night in his dream, surely a foretelling of welcome. Now the wind had dropped along the Argentine beach, rare enough at dawn, and a good omen in itself.

True, he had never taken the boat out alone before, but he was clever with motors and often helped Papa. Only, he better hurry or someone might stop him. The sun was already clearing the horizon.

Paolo paused and rocked on his heels. His sturdy body felt restricted in a wet suit. He had an open, friendly face that usually reflected a quiet happiness, but this morning he was angry and curiously sad.

Paolo didn't hesitate because of fear. He'd been afraid often enough to recognize that sinking in the stomach, the paralysis that came when his friend Luis lifted his fists. This was different. He really didn't like taking the boat without permission. And he couldn't remember disobeying Papa before, ever in his life, or wanting to.

Papa's baby, Luis said. Papa's friend was the way he felt, or had until yesterday, when his father broke his promise. And this wasn't revenge. If he had to leave, this spring was his last chance to swim with the whales, and he'd been waiting year after year—every spring since he could remember.

"When you are fourteen, you may swim with the whales," Papa had said. "I'll go with you and give you my blessing."

"But Luis has been swimming with whales for years. Two years!"

"Luis is a year older than you, and he has no father to care for him."

"But I won't be fourteen until November—four months—and the whales *leave* then." November was the beginning of summer in Argentina, the time when whales migrated north, leaving the bay at Puerto Piramides and taking their calves to the open sea.

"You have my word, Paolo."

Papa's word had always been final but dependable.

Then yesterday—without a word of warning—Papa announced that because he and Luis were the only students in eighth grade, Puerto Piramides School wouldn't offer ninth grade anymore, and he would have to send Paolo to San Francisco for school next year.

"So I've written your mother. She wants you to live

with her for the school year, wants to know her son before he's grown up and married." He'd smiled, as if this was amusing.

"To the United States? Why? I haven't even seen Mama for years." Paolo stood there on the veranda, staring at his father. "And why didn't you ask me?"

"I had to write your mother first."

"But you said we're the two musketeers; we have to stick together."

"We are sticking together. But you have to go to school. My father sent me abroad to school when I was fourteen. It's necessary for a fine education."

"No."

Papa just shook his head and turned back to his drawing. Paolo wanted to scream—talk to me! But he'd never interrupted Papa's work, and so he bit his lip and was silent.

"So, I don't care either," Paolo said now as he pushed the small outboard motorboat. Oof! Didn't move an inch, though the beach was sloped and sandy. He put his back to the stern and shoved again. No luck. Every day of his life he'd seen men push boats into the sea, throw the line in, jump aboard as their boat floated clear of the surf. He'd helped his father push theirs since he could walk. He shoved harder. And again. The skiff still wouldn't budge.

He rested a moment, leaning on the boat, looking out to sea. He saw another whale blow, the V-shaped

double blow peculiar to the southern right whales living off their Patagonian coast. There were dozens of
whales out there, mothers and newborn calves they'd
brought to nurse in the quiet bay.

Every year they returned in August, surfacing like
a fleet of submarines, and then in November, on a day
no different from any other, they mysteriously turned
and headed back out to sea, one after another. They
had been doing so for thousands of years.

When Paolo thought about it, lying in bed at night,
their migration became the greatest mystery. If he had
another life, could he come back as a whale? Papa
said he swam like he belonged to the sea. Whales were
reliable and gentle with each other, and they lived to
play. How much nicer they were than people.

"Today's the day," he said aloud, and gave the outboard motorboat a great shove. The boat shuddered,
its line pulling taut and snapping smartly.

"*Estúpido!* I've forgotten the line!" Paolo untied the
rope and pushed the boat easily.

The water felt cold on his feet. He gave a final push
before he clambered aboard, heaving himself over the
edge and tumbling inside. He sat up, checked for the
anchor and bailing can, and approached the motor
uncertainly. Miraculously, it started on the first try.
He was on his way! He set the speed on slow and
headed the skiff toward deep water. The steady purr
of the motor was reassuring.

Around him gulls dove for fish and, beneath the

surface, he saw the silver flash of dolphins looking for rockfish. Along two sides of the clam-shaped bay rose sheer cliffs, their rocky shelves awash now in the rising tide. Beyond the bay lay the Atlantic Ocean, flowing south to Antarctica.

Paolo was nearing the whales now, gigantic shadows under the water. One swam alongside, curious but careful to stay between the boat and her calf, protecting her baby. He caught his breath as the calf jumped half out of the water, breaching.

Almost pure white and so close he could see the red patches of sea lice sticking to the bumps of its head. What a treat! It was rare good fortune to see an albino calf, and this one was playful! Almost as if he were asking Paolo to play with him.

Beyond the mother and calf two more gray backs surfaced, like rocks in the ocean, dark shadows escorting his boat. They were coming to see him! He cut the motor.

The mother and calf appeared to be playing, blowing and slapping water with flippers and flukes. And the white calf breached again, leaping high and landing with a resounding splash. Paolo began to feel light-hearted, not excited exactly but privileged, a deep happiness spreading through him. A belonging.

He was eager to dive, but he made himself go over what he knew about swimming with whales first. Not that he was worried, but Luis said sometimes when whales got playful, they forgot they weighed forty tons.

Better not get too close because their callosities, the parasite-covered bumps on their heads, were sharp and could slice off a hand, had sliced off the bread vendor's thumb.

Paolo wouldn't want a stranger reaching out and poking him, so he wouldn't touch. Nor swim under a whale today because he didn't know enough yet about the currents they caused flipping those monstrous tails. Like the wake of a boat, Luis said. And Papa said that after a while, you got a sense of how to flow with the current. Besides, he wasn't sure how long he could hold his breath underwater, though he'd been practicing ever since he could walk, planning for this very swim.

Remember to drop anchor. Luis had forgotten once and spent an hour swimming after his boat.

The whale mother and her white calf were still alongside. Curious. He dropped anchor and waited in a sudden silence, water lapping around him. The whales and the birds had quieted too. Sunrise filled the sky with saffron and reflected streaks of purple on the deep blue water.

Paolo put on his goggles and climbed out of the skiff, slipping down into the cold water, striking out to swim himself warm. He was a strong swimmer and liked the feel of cutting easily through the water. He was always more graceful, more at ease in water than on land, but he couldn't remember feeling this happy, really happy. Maybe he'd already been a whale in another life. Maybe the mother and calf came alongside because they sensed some kinship with him.

He swam off to the left where the whales had been. There they were—about six feet under the water. So tempting to swim over one and peer down as if he were snorkeling, but suppose that enormous shadow suddenly surfaced? Not too good an idea. Now that he was in the water, the whales looked gigantic—colossal—without beginning or end.

He put his face in the water and set out to swim along the length of the mother whale, making an inspection of sorts. That silky dark hide looked soft and vulnerable. Parasites must hurt. And the monstrous callosities all over her head. And whiskers, that was a surprise, chin whiskers and eyebrows. And the bluish scar along her side about eight feet long—had a shark done that? Rows of deep scratches. And another long stretch of silky skin. Better avoid the tail or she might flip it.

Paolo swam off a little way, careful to keep his distance. He dove, forcing himself down to where he might see one end of the whale, and suddenly there he was—face to face with an eye—only a few yards away—this intelligent brown eye that drew him inside, as if the eye were a prism, and he was held there, staring into light that seemed to reflect a profound sadness. He felt like an intruder, a spy from an alien world. And yet the huge eye seemed gentle, accepting.

Reluctantly Paolo drew back, and when he did, the

whale also backed off and gradually submerged, sinking deeper and deeper with only the slightest movements of flippers that looked too small for the great body.

Paolo felt strange and suddenly lonely. The water around him filled with a trail of bubbles, empty bubbles. The calf had followed his mother down into the sea where Paolo couldn't go and all he'd seen, really, was one eye. All he might ever see. One mournful friendly eye.

But he hadn't been frightened! That was enough for the first day. More than enough. The greatest adventure in his life!

Paolo swam back to the boat, clambered aboard, and collapsed in the bottom, breathing hard, shaken by the wonder of that eye. He lay on his back, looking up into the sky. How long had they been eye to eye? No telling—but that whale knew something about him. And he knew something of a whale now, too, though what it was he could not have said, exactly.

He wanted to talk about that eye, though not to the fisherman who helped him pull the boat back up on the beach. He'd only laugh. He wanted to tell his father, even if it meant getting into trouble. Even if it meant confronting him, telling Papa he wouldn't leave home. He had to tell him about this swim, right now, no matter what!

Paolo looked over the beach toward the one street that made up his town. Three or four dozen houses and his and Papa's house at the end, where the street climbed up the hill. There was the bread vendor with his cart and mule already, the grocer setting out fresh vegetables, women shopping. It was late. He'd have to hurry to make it home in time for breakfast. Paolo broke into a run.

2 Paolo ran up the dirt road past the grocery store, the schoolhouse, the police station and medical clinic, glanced at the adobe *casita* where his friend Luis lived. The shutters were closed. Maybe Luis was fishing. Theirs was a fishing village, but in season men made more money showing tourists the whales, so he could be out on a charter boat.

"Buenos días, buenos días," Paolo called to everyone he met as he ran.

The wind had come up, and even in his wet suit he was getting goose pimples. Theirs was the last house on the road and the wind raked him cruelly as he raced toward it, the house Papa built for Mama because she was homesick for the hills of San Francisco.

But she left them anyway, when Paolo was a year old, driven out, she said, by a lonesome wind that never stopped. What she found she needed was the music of good conversation back home in San Francisco.

Mama hadn't taken Paolo with her then, nor when she came to visit five years ago. She sent funny letters at Christmas and his birthday, but she'd never asked him to visit. So why did Papa decide to send him halfway around the world to a mother who wanted to stay a stranger? Without even asking him!

As he neared the house, Paolo saw a strange Jeep in the driveway. Visitors again! How could he tell Papa he'd stared into a whale's eye?

Since the publication of his father's book, *Birds and Animals of Peninsula Valdes*, every naturalist in the world was dropping by to see birds and animals that lived nowhere else on earth. Flying eight thousand miles for a bowl of soup, treating Papa like a television star. So maybe he'd be in a good mood later and wouldn't get mad about the swim.

Paolo stepped onto the veranda, out of the wind. He peered around the corner and saw a beautiful blond girl about his age sitting on a whale vertebra, her face red with anger, fists clenched.

"Buenos días," he said awkwardly, shifting feet, poised to flee. Suddenly, hardly knowing what he was doing, he reached out timidly and touched her shoulder.

The girl turned slowly, staring at him, taking *everything* in, tear-filled blue eyes adding him up like she had a computer. Color rose in his cheeks. He trembled but kept a hand on her shoulder, waiting.

"You must be Paolo," she said at last. She spoke Spanish like a native, but she looked like a tourist. He took his hand away from her shoulder. A foreign girl might not be used to an Argentine's affectionate ways.

He nodded, waiting.

"I'm Samantha. Your father says we'll be in the same class. My mother's our teacher, worst luck." She looked at him with a friendly directness, not so angry now.

"Your mother's the new teacher? The señora married to the American researching whales? You're late."

"Because I ran away—to Grandma's."

"Why?"

Samantha stood up. She was as tall as Paolo, and her curly blond hair tumbled halfway down her back. She had that princess look about her—and her blue eyes flashed.

"They had to know they couldn't move away whenever they wanted and just expect me to follow. I'd worked hard at my swimming, and I could have been a champion."

Paolo stretched one arm toward the bay. "We swim here every day. I just finished," he said.

"I was competing in backstroke—for the Junior Olympics. And I would have made it, too. And now I'll never have another chance." Her voice trembled.

"Can't you try next year?"

"Not unless you have an Olympic-size pool. Ocean swimming's okay for strength but not speed. No, I'll lose a whole season and that's too much to make up."

Paolo shook his head. He wanted to say he'd help her practice, but she looked ready to cry. Maybe she was right.

"There are plenty of whales in California, you know, if Daddy just has to watch the brutes. Gray whales. Why drag the whole family down *here*?"

"Papa wants me to go, so I know just how you feel. Moving when you don't have any say." Still, maybe her father was studying *right whales*. Maybe he was doing research on their migration.

"To make me quit now when I've worked on my swimming since I was a kid! My little sister, Charley, wanted a dog, too, already named him Spoonheart, and now she can't have her pet until we go home. Six months! Mom may be an Argentine, but she's lived in California since she was my age." Samantha's voice was trembling again.

"Don't! Crying gives me hives."

"You have gorgeous brown eyes. You know? And don't look so tragic—I like to cry. You'll get used to it." Samantha smiled.

Paolo grinned back. He *must* have heard wrong. She couldn't mean *his* eyes. "Hey. After breakfast I could take you to see our whales, if you like."

"I like penguins better."

He shrugged. Penguins wouldn't migrate back to the peninsula for another three months, but why discourage her? He'd never talked to girls much, never to a pretty girl with troubles, so it was hard to know what she wanted him to say.

He reached for the door and pulled it open. With relief he saw that her parents and sister were just starting to eat. He wasn't late, then. The good smells of freshly baked croissants and coffee filled the room.

Everyone around the dining table was laughing. His father looked up. "Ah, here's Paolo now. Knows as much about whales as anyone in town, Dr. Martin. My boy talks to wild animals, too. Can call in anything you want, Charley."

"Papa!" Paolo felt himself blush. He wanted to shout, *I swam with the whales!* Instead, he slipped away to his room and changed quickly. When he came back, the redheaded little sister was waiting for him.

"Can you find me a cocker spaniel, black and white?"

"I'd rather find you an armadillo. Are you Charley?"

"My name's Charlotte, but everyone calls me Charley. My dog's going to be named Spoonheart." She looked up at Paolo, blue eyed and freckle faced, very confident.

"Samantha, do sit down and have some breakfast, dear," her mother interrupted, brow crinkled in worry, but her tone determined and cheerful.

Papa, coffeepot in hand, smiled and waved him to a place at the head of the table. He must really like these people to go to the trouble of buying croissants. Most visitors got oatmeal. Maybe because Samantha's mother was the new teacher.

"I can't hug an armadillo," Charley said.

"But they're funnier than dogs."

The little girl shook her head. "Do you have armadillos for pets?"

"Well, I feed some, but they're still wild, not pets."

"But you talk to them, right?"

"I guess," Paolo said.

"Then teach me. I'm going to be a veterinarian, and I'll need to talk to my patients."

"Oh, Charley, lay off. You haven't even started first grade and you want to talk to patients?" Samantha was still standing just inside the doorway, staring around their living room as if she couldn't believe her eyes. What was *she* looking at?

Papa's desk and a drawing easel were set up at one end of the long open room and the driftwood table they were sitting around was at the other, and there was a rattan sofa and some chairs. The checkerboard set on a whale disk, next to a telescope trained on the bay. Papa's bird sketches were pinned to the walls so he could check them against the live birds outside. So they'd look like he'd caught them in motion instead of like stuffed birds. They had a kitchen the size of a ship's galley and two small bedrooms.

"Not much to see after San Francisco."

"I knew *you'd* live in a house like this. It's so *real*, so—recycled," Samantha said.

"Recycled? A good description, I'm afraid." Papa laughed.

"Honey, look at the dolphin skeleton Dr. Alvarez put on the rafters," Dr. Martin said.

Samantha's father was going bald, so he combed each strand of hair over his bald spot like camouflage. How could he get the hairs to stay? And why bother?

"Did you have to boil the bones like Daddy did with our whale disks? They stunk up the whole neighborhood."

"Samantha, don't tell family secrets. Hugh would keep a pod of whales in our backyard if he could, Dr. Alvarez." Samantha's mother turned her entire head when she looked at someone, like an owl would. Otherwise, she looked like Samantha, only wrinkled. Another quarter of a century and you'll earn your wrinkles too, Papa always said.

"I'd like to pick your brain about these whales one day," Dr. Martin said, fixing Paolo with his pale blue eyes, sailor's eyes.

"Well, as a matter of fact, this morning I—" Paolo said, and then stopped. Everyone was looking at him.

"This morning?"

"The whales are back," Paolo muttered.

"We all know that, Son." Papa grinned. "What else?"

"There's an albino calf."

"Oh, I'd like to see that baby," said Dr. Martin.

"Anything else, Paolo?" Papa asked.

Paolo felt himself blushing again. Okay, it would serve Papa right if he told. Why not let Samantha know he swam eye to eye with a whale? But Papa would say he was sneaky, telling it out like this when he couldn't get mad. And he'd be right. "Dolphins," he said.

"How about dinosaurs? Were there really dinosaurs here, like Dad says?"

"Never laid eyes on one, Samantha, but every once in a while we find a few of their bones, enough to prove they were here. Nothing major. But archaeologists come in here and find fairly well-preserved skeletons every now and then, so I guess there were quite a few, all right. Mostly the smaller earlier species," Papa said.

"See, I told you so," said Charley. "And I'll find *Tyrannosaurus rex*, so there."

"Mo-ther!"

"Charley, do simmer down, dear."

Samantha looked out over the windswept land. "It's so empty, creepy enough for dinosaurs," she whispered to Paolo. "Do you have any dinosaur bones?"

Paolo grinned. "I've got a couple of bones that don't look like they came from a cow or a sheep. Papa's going to send them up to La Plata to be authenticated for me." Luis's mama said they brought good luck, dinosaur bones, so it was always a tug-of-war, Papa wanting to send them off for "science" and Paolo trying to keep them for good luck.

"Can I—"

"No, Charley, you can't have one," her father said firmly.

"I only want to see one," Samantha whispered.

Paolo grinned and went to get the two disks from the windowsill. They were each five or six inches across and about three inches high.

"Just old gray rocks," Charley said, picking one up. "Hey, it's heavy. I have to use both hands."

"They've fossilized," Paolo said, sounding defensive to himself. Maybe they were only old rocks. When he'd seen them, they'd seemed so terribly old, etched and worn by the winds of a million years.

"Like stone lace around the edges," Samantha said, cupping one in her hand and running one finger around the edge again and again.

"Trying to make the genie come out of the lamp?" Paolo asked.

Samantha looked up and laughed. "Come out, come out—oh, mighty dinosaur—emerge and live once more." She chanted the words slowly and in a low deep voice.

"Not if you're carnivorous!" Charley cried out.

"He only eats girls under eight. Ten-der meat," Samantha continued in the same spooky voice.

"Hmmm, interesting bone," said Samantha's father.

"Well, maybe only a huge cow—but since they'd fossilized . . ."

"Will you take me there, where you found these? Soon?" Samantha asked.

"They only have one channel on TV," Charley said, eager to change the subject.

"What's the matter? Scared of a bone, oh brave veterinarian?" asked Samantha, waving the disk at Charley.

"That's enough, girls."

"They don't even have a movie theater," Charley continued, backing away from the disk.

Samantha looked startled and handed the disk back to Paolo as if she'd suddenly lost interest.

Papa grinned at Samantha. Well, wait until Papa found out where *he'd* been this morning. Eyeball to eyeball with a whale. The last of the dinosaurs, that's what whales were.

But you could see why Papa was so happy. The Martins were a family, and it did feel good to have them here, all talking at once and laughing together. Señora Martin was saying she'd been born in Buenos Aires, so teaching in Spanish would be a pleasure.

She was listening to Papa's rundown on the school as if he were the Pope. She laughed easily, asking questions that showed she knew a lot about the peninsula and the school.

Paolo felt the talk flowing around him, as if he was in the eye of the storm. Just like this morning out on the bay after he cut the motor, watching the whales come alongside. He wanted to plunge into the conversation and tell the Martins and Papa how it was swimming with the whales so he wouldn't lose the feeling. He wanted to bring that sympathetic eye back and prove it hadn't been a dream. He wanted to describe that whale's eye!

"Tell me, Dr. Alvarez, how many students will I have?"

"Twenty-five to thirty, Señora, fourth grade through eighth grade. We're so grateful that you could take over while our teacher's out on maternity leave."

"I'll try. Is this a one-room school?"

"You mean I have to be in the same classroom with Charley? You can't make me—horrible!"

"Samantha will tell all the kids I'm a pest and then no one will like me," Charley said in a resigned voice.

"Relax, ladies. First through third grade are in one room. Fourth through eighth, your mother's classes, are in another. You won't be together," Papa assured them.

"Whew, what a narrow escape," said Samantha.

"You've saved my life, Dr. Alvarez," said Charley.

"How many people does your town have?" Señora Martin asked, shushing her daughters.

"Less than a hundred, mostly fishermen, but you'll draw students from the surrounding *estancias*, too," Papa said.

"May Paolo and I be excused?"

Señora Martin nodded absently, and Samantha pulled Paolo away from the table and out onto the windy veranda without saying a word. Behind them he heard Charley asking to be excused and being told to finish eating first.

"Now then," Samantha said, sitting on the whale vertebra again.

"Now then, what?"

"Talk to me. What did you say about moving away?"

"Okay. Remember, you asked. Papa wants to send me to a mama I hardly know in San Francisco. I won't go."

"Reverse of me, huh? When?" Samantha asked, and, finding it wouldn't be until after she returned, launched into the wonders of San Francisco, California. "And I'll personally show you everything."

"Hey, wait a minute, Samantha. You didn't want to come here, right? Well, I don't want to leave home either. I thought you'd understand," he muttered.

Samantha stood up then, and she looked embarrassed. "Sorry. Are you going because of your dad's job too?"

"No, just me, to my mother's. When she was here five years ago, she and Papa spent most of the time arguing. She and I are strangers."

"What did they argue about?"

"Mama wanted Papa to try living in San Francisco, but he said he was Argentine. I hate thinking about it."

"It sounds awful!"

"Why should he want me to go when he wouldn't?"

Samantha nodded but said nothing. The silence between them seemed to stretch like a rubber band.

"Isn't it strange," Samantha finally said. "You're an Argentine half-breed and I'm an American half-breed. We have a lot in common. You know? So—bring on the whales."

He was getting used to the sudden shifts in her conversation. You'd never get bored talking with Samantha. "Come on, then. Maybe we'll see the white calf, the albino, very rare. You'll love him."

"You might as well know now that I don't love anything just because someone tells me to. I make up my own mind. Why should I love this white calf?" she asked, but without giving him a chance to answer rushed on. "So tell me about the other kids in our class."

"There's only one. Luis."

"Only three of us in the whole eighth grade? And

I'm the only girl! That's a new one. How will I like that? A lot's going to depend on you, Paolo. And this Luis, of course. What's he like?"

Paolo shrugged off that loaded question. "You can call me Gordo. Everyone does."

"Hey, don't change the subject. I asked about Luis. When do I meet him?"

3 As they talked, Paolo and Samantha walked down to a cliff overlooking the bay. They sat on a broad flat rock and watched a dozen whales breaching, playing, napping, rising like islands out of the blue water.

"It's better than Marine World! Let's find this Luis and we'll have the whole eighth grade," Samantha said after a while.

"He's fishing." Luis would be in by now, but Paolo didn't intend to share Samantha. He'd never met anyone who asked so many questions about whales or dinosaur traces. She was more interesting than the girls on the peninsula. He looked into her blue eyes and felt himself blush.

"Hmmmm? Okay, tell me where White Calf goes when he leaves here. Give me a whale's year," she demanded.

"You have to know it all in one day? Scientists like your dad are only finding out now. By tracing the callosities, the bumps on each whale's head, they can photograph them as they travel and trace their migration patterns."

"You mean White Calf's bumps on the head are different than his mother's?"

"Right."

Finally she asked the question he'd worried about, looking up at him with trusting eyes. "So, do you swim with them like I've read about? When can I go with you?"

Paolo knew it was time to go home. There was no way he could take Samantha swimming with the whales and no way he could tell her he'd gone or say he hadn't, either. "I don't know. Very dangerous," he mumbled.

"I can swim circles around you, Gordo. Don't try and put me off."

When he got home, Paolo studied his face in the hall mirror. The wide-set brown eyes and curly brown hair were all right, and his skin was clearer than Luis's, but the pudgy cheeks and the almost double chin must be disgusting, from a girl's point of view. "*Bueno*, time to tell Papa. Do it now," he told himself in the mirror.

They took turns making supper, and this afternoon, his father had *puchero* simmering on the stove. Lamb stew was easy to prepare and a favorite meal and tended to put Papa in a good mood. It would be a fine time to talk, except that he was reading an article by

Samantha's father, grunting now and again in approval. So Paolo waited.

Papa didn't mind being interrupted, but usually they played a game of checkers before dinner and did their talking then, in English, so Paolo could talk if he visited his American mother someday. They'd always talked English with checkers. Maybe Papa had always planned to send him to Mama?

"Papa?"

"Have a good time, Son? I understand your friend Samantha plays *chess* with her father," he said, putting aside the article and setting up the checkers.

The *viejo*, or old one as he sometimes called Papa, loved chess but he was a grandmaster, one of the best chess players in the world, and couldn't help winning. After about a year of being beaten in five moves, Paolo refused to play chess anymore. He let his father choose, though—checkers, Chinese checkers, or dominoes. About twice a year Papa chose Chinese checkers, but they'd never yet played dominoes.

"Good for Samantha. Red or black, Papa?"

"Black." He sighed.

"She ran away to show her parents they couldn't just drag her away from her swimming whenever they wanted."

"Not very considerate of her."

"Only to her grandmother's. But why should we have to leave home for our father's convenience?"

"Us? Some things in this world you have to do, Son—for your education, to know your mother, certainly not for my convenience. Your move."

This conversation was not going the way Paolo planned. *Estúpido* to get Papa mad if he wanted him to approve swimming with the whales. "Mama was here. I know her."

The older man peered across the board from under bushy eyebrows, with a curious half-smile that lit up his gray eyes. "Aha, I am jumping you. You should watch—"

"So that's why you were smiling!"

"Can't a man smile in his own house?"

"My house too, though you want to kick me out." The words were out, and though Paolo knew it was the worst thing he could do, he plunged on. "Listen, let me stay home. Please! We can send for correspondence courses."

"You need exposure to your own species, Paolo."

The kindness in Papa's eyes was annoying, belittling somehow. But he'd gotten careless with his checkers. "Man, the most dangerous animal, moves! See, I jump you here—*and* here! Your move, Papa."

"Lord, I must be going blind."

Paolo leaned on one elbow and waited. Papa sipped coffee and studied the board, finally moving so he put Paolo's king in jeopardy. Wind rattled the roof, making it hard to concentrate. Seals barked on the bay.

Paolo moved.

Papa grunted approval. Paolo's move had blocked his.

"I prefer whales to my own kind. And I have Luis," Paolo said finally.

"Yes, I can see why whales might be preferable to Luis. But how about meeting more Samanthas? After all, whales migrate and come back here every year. I went abroad to school when I was your age. Why can't you? King me."

Paolo kicked the whale disk that served as the table but not hard enough to jar the board. He was tempted to point out that man wasn't a migrating animal, but that was risky. He moved farther from the new king, but before taking his hand off the checker he saw the mistake and backtracked, looking up to see if the *viejo* objected.

The older man grinned. "Used your head. Good. Samantha like the whales?"

"She said they made her believe in history. Papa, this morning—" He sat on his hands to keep them from trembling. He had to get things clear between them. But how to begin?

"She met Luis yet?"

Paolo shook his head glumly. Tomorrow they started school, and barring blood poisoning or appendicitis, there was no way to keep them from meeting. "Why so slow? Your move, Papa."

"Sorry, just thinking, Son, just thinking. I was glad

to meet your new teacher, Señora Martin, and her family. Mama would have liked her. They could have had those long conversations Leonora missed so."

That made the fourth time Papa had voluntarily mentioned Mama since she came to visit five years ago. Paolo had been eight at the time and had hoped they'd be a family again, but Mama said only if they could live in California and Papa said only if they lived in Puerto Piramides. Paolo had been afraid Papa might go. The loving way his father said Leonora now gave him goose pimples!

Then Papa jumped two men.

Then Paolo jumped two, one a king. Maybe he could win this game! Papa got up to get another cup of coffee, which meant the subject of Mama was closed.

"Son?"

"Yes?" His father was spooning sugar, four teaspoonsful, into the black coffee. He didn't gain weight, so why should his son?

"What about this morning?" Papa asked.

"This morning?"

"You were trying to tell me something and I interrupted. What is it?" He set the coffee cup on the floor and sat down, his gray eyes on Paolo's face.

"I forget."

"All right."

"No, wait—I want to tell you. I went swimming with the whales this morning, Papa. I couldn't wait for my birthday. There's not enough time."

"You *whaaat*?"

"I—swam—with the—whales."

"Stupid damn luck you lived to tell the tale. Luis bully you into it?"

"I went alone. He doesn't even know."

"So you risked your life because you were mad at me about going away to school. I'm ashamed of you." Papa stood up and paced the room, muttering.

Paolo flushed and hung his head. "No, not mad— hurt. And worried. From what you say, I won't be here when the whales return."

"Respect the size of those creatures, if nothing else! Learn their ways and how to swim their currents, like you study *any* wild animal. Haven't I taught you *anything*?"

Paolo watched his father pacing the floor and running his hands through curly hair like his own but gray. He wanted to run to him, to promise never again, but he couldn't. Nothing had ever felt so wonderful, and there was no way he wouldn't go out with those whales again.

"But I did everything you taught me. Everything."

"Taught you? A few pointers, nothing to what you need to know. Good Lord!"

Out in the bay the whales would be taking long dives in the late afternoon, grazing the ocean for plankton, their great mouths open. "Then teach me," Paolo said very quietly.

"I can't spend my days following you around like a wet nurse."

Paolo trembled. He bit his lip to keep from answering back. They almost never disagreed. What could he say?

"What I do is for your own good—both with the whales and your education. *Why* can't you trust me?"

"Why can't you trust *me*?"

"Because you do damn fool stunts like going off half-*loco*, swimming with ten-ton whales."

Papa was pacing the floor, his face crimson, a coffee cup still in one hand. He stopped and stood staring out the window, then turned abruptly, facing Paolo. "God knows, I'll be lonely rattling around this place without you."

"You'll miss me?"

"Why not?" Papa managed a wry grin. They looked at each other a long moment. "All right. All right! Well, if you're so hell-bent to swim with whales, let's get started. Pronto. Into your wet suit, yes, now! Grab your snorkel and goggles. And here's lesson number one. You never, never swim with whales alone—a flip of the tail and you're done for. Leave the checkers. This could mean your life."

"But you would miss me? I'm not a nuisance?"

"Of course—but it's getting late, Son. We can talk later. You'd better get a move on if we're going out on that bay before the sun goes down." Suddenly Papa became a whirling dervish, turning off the stew, throwing on his wet suit, packing sweatshirts.

Paolo hurried into his wet suit and jogged down the road after his father, buffeted by a cold wind. Papa loved to jog. But ten minutes ago he was in a fury about the swim, because he hadn't been there directing every move. So why should Papa send him halfway around the world alone? Papa could teach him. It didn't make sense.

Paolo panted as he tried to keep up. He should've taken a drink of water.

Puffing badly, he caught up only when his father had already pushed their skiff halfway across the beach. The day was blustery, but they were able to launch the boat. They skimmed it through the surf, jumped in, and started the motor. Neither tried to speak—between the wind and the motor it was too noisy. They were on their way. He was coming out to the whales a second time in one day. They spotted tails and blow sprays over toward the cliffs, and his father headed toward them.

"Papa, I saw the albino calf this morning over on the other side." Paolo pointed off to the right, where he'd caught a glimpse of a pale back and a darker one rising out of the water.

His father turned right but cut the motor short of where Paolo thought he'd seen the whales and let down the anchor. "We don't want to be chasing them, making them uneasy," he said in the sudden silence. "If they get curious, they'll come to us."

And if they don't, we can sit out here until hell freezes over, Paolo thought. The whales were breaching and slapping the water with their tails.

Papa pointed at two sprays of water, the blows coming closer. Could it possibly be them? Paolo wanted to say he'd been eyeball to eyeball with the white calf, but Papa wouldn't think that had been too smart. He listened to the shearlings and gulls, the steady whine of the wind, the silver flash of dolphins playing in the last rays of sunshine. "Another hour and the sun'll be gone," said Papa.

Suddenly a pair of right whales surfaced not fifty feet from their boat. He could even hear the soft *whoosh-whoosh* of their breathing. The albino calf! The calf tossed its tail and dove under the boat. Its shadow, so big they seemed to be floating over land, hung under them for long minutes. Then, ever so gently, the whale calf rubbed his back against their keel. Paolo could see the callosities on his head shining through the clear water. "He's the one I saw this morning, Papa."

"Frisky little devil. Watch out for that calf's tail, Son! If you *ever* see the tail coming down on you, dive. Immediately! You don't want to get crushed between the boat and one of those two-ton tails."

Paolo nodded, watching *this* whale ever so carefully

dip its tail and remove any danger. Then the calf rolled to one side and blew. The mist from his blow poured over them, leaving a smell like warm fur, as the calf circled and swam off to its mother. Then it breached and dove, coming up a few minutes later on the other side of their boat.

"That's a lively one, your friend, showing off," Papa said uneasily.

"Think so?" Paolo grinned. If only he could tell about being eye to eye with the calf this morning, but Papa was sure to explode. "I call him White Calf."

"Whales aren't dogs, Paolo."

They were quiet, watching the white whale skim ever so slowly under their boat, scratch his back on the keel, and return to the mother, who called to her calf in a voice like a soft foghorn. He was playing—breaching, leaping half out of the water and sinking back, playing in slow motion, breaching again and again.

"Lovely time of day," Papa said, his face gentle.

"Let's get going," Paolo begged.

"This whale is friendly and playful—but don't ever forget he already weighs several tons. And he doesn't know his own strength. Get caught in the currents he makes breaching and you'll feel a riptide like a tsunami. But if you do, go with it, the same as any other rip. And most important of all, don't give his mother any reason to worry. She's very protective. Never swim to a whale. Let her come to you. And not too close. Understand?"

"Yes, Papa. *Vamos? Por favor.*"

"Don't forget your snorkel and goggles and be quiet." After checking the calf and the mother for the hundredth time, Papa finally let himself over the side.

Paolo followed. Even with the wet suit the water was cold, and he was glad to strike out swimming after Papa.

Soon they were only a few yards from the mother's head. Below her he could see the calf, its pale hide shining through the water. He and his father floated easily, peering through goggles, the late-afternoon sun warming their backs. Paolo looked up to find the mother's dark eyes regarding him curiously.

For some minutes they remained like that, studying each other, so that what Paolo would remember was the strange bowl formation of the callosities across her forehead. Then, perhaps satisfied, the mother sank slowly into the water without churning riptides, and emitting a curious whumping sound, she and the calf disappeared from view.

His father tapped him on the foot, pointing toward the boat. Paolo swam after him, reluctant to go, but filled with the wonder of what he'd seen. Now Papa had also been eye to eye with a whale. They could talk.

However, when they were once again in the boat,

Papa's smile was tight. "Didn't like the look of that whale sizing us up," he said. "They can get mighty protective of their young. Never, never, never come out here alone."

"I said I wouldn't," Paolo snapped. Wouldn't Papa ever stop lecturing? Didn't he see *anything out here*?

"Just be sure you remember," Papa replied shortly, pulling up the anchor, starting the motor, and heading the skiff toward shore. The wind whistled at their backs, pushing them back to land.

The sun was just sinking below the horizon, leaving a red sky, as they secured the little boat once again on the beach. "Did you see that whale's eye?" Paolo asked.

"Yes, entirely too well, considering she has a calf."

Paolo sighed. Papa's lessons were better than nothing, but he sure managed to take the fun out of it.

Well, it was only August. School started tomorrow. Anything could happen in five months, before the term ended and the whales left. Anything.

LUIS

4 "I hate having Mom for a teacher. Like I'm her little girl. I'm a free and independent student," Samantha told Paolo in their classroom before school.

But she was, she added, enchanted with the two-room schoolhouse overlooking the bay. And the pretty doctor's wife who taught Charley's first grade through third in the other room. Her mother taught fourth through eighth in their room. She liked the way each grade sat together at a square wooden table.

"And me the only girl between two guys. And I love having tea and toast at school in the morning. So civilized."

Paolo was showing Samantha Whale Camp, where she would be living, on a wall map. Out of the corner of his eye he saw Luis walk in.

Luis let out a long, low whistle.

Samantha whirled, and Paolo could tell she was surprised by the way her eyes widened and seemed even bluer.

"You *must* be Luis," she said, looking into his eyes.

"Of course."

It was easy for Paolo to see how Luis must look to Samantha. He had a tango dancer's build, tall and slim, and he combed his black hair straight back. And girls liked his eyes—brown with curious yellow flecks and, like a cat's eyes, they gleamed when he was excited. You look into those eyes and drown, Luis's old girlfriend had told Paolo.

"But has an angel come to walk on earth?" asked Luis. "Where have you been hiding her, Gordo? Introduce us, *amigo*."

"This is Samantha. Her mother is our new teacher," Paolo said with a shrug and a deep sadness. Was he going to lose Samantha now, the only girl he'd *ever* been able to talk to? And to Luis, who used to be his best friend? Paolo and Luis had played together all their lives, riding across the peninsula from dawn until dinner, watching nesting penguins, competing to see the first returning whales every August and the newborn elephant seals in October. Luis was a year older and had the eyes of a hawk. Paolo had the instincts of a tracker and read enough to know what they were seeing. Together they made a good team.

Then one day last winter Luis said, "Go home, Gordo. I must be the man now and buy food and medicine for Mama. She's too sick to work. I've no time to play anymore."

Just like that. Luis always had a temper, but since

that one day he'd turned mean, like a bull elephant seal.

Now Luis was inviting Samantha to go horseback riding after school. He had time to play with her, apparently.

"If Paolo wants to," Samantha said, as if she didn't care one way or the other.

"Maybe Gordo has other fish to fry," Luis suggested, his eyes narrowing.

Paolo said nothing.

"No, Gordo promised me," she said.

Promised her? When?

"All right. We'll all go riding. Right, Gordito?"

Señora Martin called school to order with a big cowbell, and while students were rushing around finding their seats, Luis grabbed Paolo's arm.

"Forget her, Gordo. She's not for you, *chico*," he whispered.

Paolo felt sick to his stomach. Luis was warning him. He groped his way to his seat, next to Samantha and across the table from Luis. Well, he'd go riding! He'd go anywhere Samantha went, whether Luis liked it or not.

After school Paolo, Luis, and Samantha set out on horseback to explore Peninsula Valdes. Paolo rode his faithful brown Pancho. Luis had a black stallion, and Samantha rode Papa's white mare. Criollo horses, short and stocky, with powerful chests and massive hooves. Built for endurance. Samantha called them Sumo wrestler horses.

"Let's head for Whale Camp. *Vamos?*"

"Luis, that's a four-hour ride. Be too dark to see a thing before we get there," Paolo said.

"I'm a city girl. A four-hour ride would kill me."

"But I wanted to be the one to show you your new home," Luis persisted. He brought his horse up next to Samantha's and placed one hand on her saddle. "Why not, beautiful?"

She flushed angrily. "I said I don't want to. I don't know this horse yet. And Mom wants me back at the Hotel Tourista before dark."

Luis frowned, then shrugged and wheeled his horse away.

"Why not head inland and show her a guanaco herd? Maybe we'll see some maras or ostriches," Paolo suggested.

"Show me where the dinosaurs lived," said Samantha.

Luis didn't answer. He knew Whale Camp was too far. Just too *macho* to back down. After all, he'd spent half the day whispering across the table—telling Samantha how he took tourists out on the bay to see the whales, swam with whales, supported his mother. She'd turn to Paolo, and he had to nod. It was true. She still seemed skeptical, but she had promised to go fishing with Luis on Saturday. So he had nothing to complain about.

"Mom needs me home, to help with the moving. Doesn't this dusty wind ever stop? I'm washing my hair every day."

"Papa says this wind's been blowing since the dinosaurs waded ashore."

"*Stegosaurus* has my sympathy."

"*Bueno.* Beautiful, we go back early for your mama." Luis smiled, smug. The moving gave him a way out of the Whale Camp trip without backing down. And Samantha smiled back this time, a wonderful smile Paolo hadn't seen before.

Paolo sighed and looked out over windswept, barren land to the horizon. To Samantha, it must seem a badlands strewn with spiky bushes and fossil bones, but he saw a desert about to burst into spring bloom. In another week those tiny red, yellow, and blue buds would pop open. They were blooming early this year.

Samantha sniffed the air. "When you really look, these bushes have the sweetest flowers. Those little red buds."

"Papa says there are two kinds of people, those who see the flowers on the bushes and those who don't—you pass, Samantha," Paolo said, laughing.

"Thanks. It's wild out here. Primeval. How far away did you find those dinosaur disks?"

"We'll pass the meadow. Guanacos use it some. And I've seen petrified paw prints there, too."

Suddenly Luis jerked his black stallion, and for a moment he looked ready to charge. Paolo's horse shied. Then Luis pulled up short, his horse pawing the air.

"*Estúpido! I* asked her to come riding! What are you, anyhow, a damn foreigner?"

They stared at each other. Then Paolo understood. He'd fallen into English without thinking, and Luis, knowing no English, thought he was showing off. Out of the corner of his eye Paolo could see Samantha frowning. She gave them each a long look and finally turned back to Luis.

Luis saw the frown too, and turning toward her, quickly smiled. "Samantha?" he asked, his voice gentle.

"Maybe a *Brontosaurus* once ate these little red flowers," she said in Spanish again, blushing, leaning over to look at a small barrel cactus.

Luis leaned down and picked the blossom and handed it to her. "Maybe *Allosaurus;* I think he was here. But I'd rather talk about you, no?" Then he touched spurs to his horse's flanks and took off at a gallop. For a few minutes the dust was smothering, and when it cleared, he was only a small figure on the horizon.

"Touchy, isn't he?" Samantha commented.

Paolo shrugged. "*Macho.* A kind of pride we have

here." He'd never been able to talk about Luis or how he changed last year, even to Papa. Not because of the fear. More a competition stuck in his craw and in Luis's. Maybe it had started long ago, when he'd find a shell or a rock and Luis wanted it. But there were so many shells, who cared?

After they started school, they even did homework together. Sometimes Luis would get so mad if Paolo understood and he didn't that he'd throw books, papers, pencils, the works sky high and stomp on them when they fell. But he also helped Paolo with math. No, Luis had always been fiery, but it was only this last year, since his mama got sick and he went to work, that he'd been getting mean. He'd begun pushing Paolo around, calling him spoiled and Papa's baby, couldn't spare one minute to talk. He'd got to feeling Luis couldn't bear having him around. He didn't know why.

"Is he your best friend?"

"Yes and no. We've always lived close by, and the other boys live on *estancias* outside of town." Paolo flushed. He didn't want to sound self-pitying. "It's all right."

"Sure—I'm alone here too. Maybeth or Tony can't ring me up from San Francisco, that's for sure." She sighed.

"I'd—like to be your friend." Paolo couldn't believe he'd said the words out loud. And he'd embarrassed her. She was blushing. *Estúpido*. People became friends; they didn't *ask*, like they were asking for a piece of cake.

Even Samantha's laugh sounded surprised. She didn't answer for a little, thinking it over. "Well— why not? You need a friend and so do I. Yes, I appoint you Samantha's friend," she said softly, touching his head lightly with her riding whip.

They rode for a while without saying anything, as if they'd already said more than enough, leaving themselves out on some risky limb. And he didn't want her thinking he *needed* a friend, like some charity case. And yet he knew she'd meant it. They'd be friends.

As they climbed into brush country he scanned the horizon for guanacos and ostriches. Over the dwarfed bushes and the bones whitened by sand and time and scattered by the wind, they could see a long way.

"This country. I bet it looked this way to the cavemen," Samantha said finally.

"Only marshier. Papa says the earliest dinosaurs lived here, before they got so huge, and they needed water."

"I've been looking for a bone, but I guess you need to be on foot. Will you help me someday?"

"Any day! But I'm no expert. You might be settling for a cow shinbone."

"And what on earth are *those*?" asked Samantha, pointing at four stocky brown animals sitting on their haunches nearby. They had heads like dogs and bodies like rabbits. "Space-age rabbits or something?"

"Those are maras, biggest guinea pigs in the world."

"Charley could cuddle them. Those hooves could be mean, though."

"She might get a nasty bite. They're too shy to tame. They'll race a car, though—keep pace with our Jeep for miles."

"Unreal! Will they race our horses? Uh-oh, here he comes. Batman returns," Samantha said, pointing at a cloud of dust that half-obscured Luis, who was galloping toward them, causing the crouching maras to scurry for cover.

"Biggest herd of guancaos I've ever seen. Follow me. Hurry!" he called out as he rode up to them and then turned, pulling his horse about so abruptly it shied and almost threw him before he galloped back into his own dust.

"Hey, wait a minute. What's a guanaco?" Samantha yelled after Luis, brushing dust off her clothing.

"Know about llamas?" Paolo asked, grinning.

"Sure, Peruvian pack animals movie stars like to raise."

"Oh, yeah? Well, a guanaco is like a llama, except it's darker, more of a cinnamon color, and a little bigger. They're cousins to the camel, but they don't have humps. Long neck, big eyes, skinny legs—Papa says God made them up out of spare parts. Like maras, the only place in the world they live is here in Patagonia."

"I believe you. Moon craters over the next hill? Guanacos, ostriches, maras. How'll I keep them straight?"

"A guanaco's an animal, an ostrich is a bird, and a mara's a rodent." Paolo spurred his horse and cried, "Luis! Stop or you'll spook the herd."

They'd reached the crest of a dry outcropping looking over a valley carpeted in grass, and below them grazed at least fifty guanacos. Small ostriches danced around the edges of the herd.

"Ooooohh—beautiful, so elegant," Samantha whispered.

"Ostriches always look like they think they're superior," muttered Luis.

Paolo was trying to see the guanacos as Samantha must be seeing them—woolly, reddish-brown animals with long arched necks and big dark eyes. Wary eyes. Then he heard a warning cry, a high-pitched whinny. "The herd's caught our scent. How do you like guanacos, Samantha?"

"Broiled," said Luis.

"The ostriches really *are* ballerinas in their fluffy tutus, aren't they? Like in *Fantasia*," Samantha said, ignoring Luis.

"Guanacos'll spit in your eye, blind you," said Luis.

Paolo grinned. "Or ballerinas are like ostriches?"

"Well, their homegrown tutus are elegant."

She and Paolo laughed easily together.

"*I* found them for *you*, beautiful," Luis said.

Samantha nodded, still watching the ostriches through her binoculars. She turned back toward Paolo. "They even go up on their toes—extraordinary!"

"Proves dancers copy ostriches, that's all."

"Listen! *I said I found them for you, Samantha.*"

She turned and gave Luis a long, appraising look. "Really?"

Luis broke away then and rode pell-mell down into the valley, whipping his horse and yelling at the top of his lungs. The ostriches scurried off, half-flying, skimming the earth, squawking shrilly. The guanacos seemed to freeze, startled, ears abruptly pricked up, long necks tensed, waiting. Heads held proudly, they looked at Luis.

Then one animal gave a whinnying laugh, then a dozen, and they took off, cantering back into the spiky bushes on the horizon, Luis in hot pursuit. Another five minutes and it was as though they had never been there. The pasture was empty except for Luis, a solitary figure walking his horse, looking bewildered as he often did after an outburst. Luis, who delighted in the unpredictable guanacos. He looked so alone.

"Hmm, temper, temper," murmured Samantha, and then, pointing, "What's that?"

"Luis?"

"I see Luis. No, the animal down there, to the left. There, see?" She handed him the binoculars.

Carefully he swept the area and made out a baby

guanaco, much the color of the tawny grassland. It wobbled about nervously, making sad little bleating noises.

"Not more than a couple days old—a *chulengo*, a baby guanaco—the mother'll come back for him after we leave."

"For sure? Charley's dying for a pet," Samantha said, slipping down off her horse.

"They spit with the speed of a bullet and aim for the eyes, like Luis said."

"Oh, come on, Gordo. Maras bite, guanacos spit. Give us a break."

"Besides, the mother'll come back and she won't like it if she smells your scent on him," said Paolo, watching Luis swing up onto his horse and head slowly back toward them, straight and slim and angry and ashamed.

"Are you *sure* that mother will come back?"

Paolo nodded, still watching Luis warily. He dismounted and stood with Samantha, who was watching the baby guanaco. "He's better off with his herd."

"Says who?"

"We're even," Luis told Samantha as he joined them a few minutes later, swinging gracefully down off his horse.

"What for?"

"You were rude to me."

Samantha regarded Luis steadily. "You interrupted

me first. Anyhow, we're even, drop it. Okay? How about this baby guanaco as a pet for my little sister?"

Luis looked at Paolo and shrugged. "If the mother doesn't come back," he said. "I'll see."

"You *know* they can't tame a guanaco, Luis!"

"If you say so." Without another word, Luis remounted and took the lead. They rode back single file under the setting sun. No one spoke. They each needed time alone, Paolo thought. The land, so desolate earlier, filled with the quiet twittering of birds settling for the night. Paolo looked at Luis's back and worried.

"Don't forget the dinosaur bone, Gordo, and the guanaco, Luis," Samantha said as the boys left her at the Hotel Tourista.

They doubled back up the street. As they approached the run-down adobe *casita* where Luis and his mother lived, the older boy reined in and waited. When Paolo came alongside, Luis took hold of his reins with one hand. With the other he grabbed Paolo's hair and yanked, hard.

"*Qué pasa* with you? *Qué loco!*" The words burst from Paolo.

"Listen, Papa's baby, stop showing off! You don't understand one little thing about me. You never did."

"So tell me." Paolo winced in pain.

Then like lightning, Luis brought his other fist up under Paolo's chin with a punch that made him bite his tongue.

"Damn it! Stop it, Luis. You've gone too far this time!"

"Lay off Samantha! Understand! You have everything else! Leave her alone."

Paolo shook his head, stunned by the attack. Luis had never socked him before. "You're crazy," he said, too proud to spit out blood where Luis could see it. *Basta!*

"Leave her alone, Gordo!" Then Luis wheeled his horse and left, riding down to his house.

Paolo spit blood. His jaw throbbed, pain coming in wave after wave. He spurred his horse. He wasn't going to stay and let Luis see him cry. Or throw up. Would there be bruises? Would his tongue need stitches? What on earth could he tell Papa?

THE RESCUE

5 Paolo told his father that the swelling purple bruise on his chin came from falling off his horse.

"Then Luis rides too damn fast for you. Lucky you didn't lose a couple of teeth," Papa grumbled, preparing an ice pack.

"*Sí*, too fast," Paolo whispered as the cold pack intensified the pain until he thought he'd pass out. Still, it had been comforting when the *viejo* felt so sorry for him that he made dinner, even though it was Paolo's turn.

By the next morning his swelling had gone down some, but pain was a constant reminder that Luis was no longer a friend who could be trusted. Perhaps no longer a friend he wanted, and this hurt more than his jaw.

It was Saturday. Samantha was going fishing with Luis, and in the afternoon the family would be moving out to Whale Camp. With luck she wouldn't see his face until Monday and he should look better by then.

After breakfast Paolo found himself walking down the road toward the cliff overlooking Luis's favorite fishing spot. *"Estúpido, estúpido,"* he muttered, bracing himself against the wind, dust seeping into every pore and stinging his bruised chin. He hated himself for trying to find Samantha and Luis, but he couldn't help it.

He stopped on the cliff overlooking the rocks where he and Luis often went fishing and looked down to the water.

Sure enough. There they were. Sitting together on a shelf of rock jutting out over the bay. Samantha's blond head bent toward Luis's sharp dark profile. The sound of their laughter carried over the surf.

Luis was cutting bait. Samantha held one of the reels he was so proud of—an orange juice can, fit with a wooden handle and with fishing cord wrapped around it. She was tying hooks on the end of the cord.

But it was the expression on Luis's face that held Paolo. Such an easy smile. How could Samantha help smiling at this Luis? No trace of the tense, ready-to-pounce alertness that had become habitual with Luis since he'd gone to work for the tourist agency a year ago. He'd disappeared into that boat, always away taking tourists to fish or to see the whales when Paolo knocked on his door. He could get off when he wanted to, though. Like today.

He was spying. Any minute one of them could look up and find him. Luis would have every right to be mad. Still, he couldn't pull himself away. He used to see Luis this *simpático*—with this easy smile. Days when they'd go fishing, exploring, hunting for ostrich eggs, swimming in the lagoon. Luis'd been rough but not cruel, and he was so daring. They'd had many adventures together.

Watching them, Paolo felt loss more than jealousy. He'd been missing Luis and found Samantha and now maybe neither of them would need him. What if he just climbed on down and said, "*Hola*, I've come to fish with you."

But he knew better, even before he had gotten socked. Samantha might grin that lazy teasing grin and act happy to see him. And Luis would go crazy. Something about him drove Luis *loco* these days.

"He's bitter. And he has to work. I don't want you around him anymore," Papa had said when he was giving excuses for sending Paolo around the world to San Francisco.

"*Caramba! Caramba!*" Paolo yelled the forbidden word into the wind. Far below, Samantha and Luis still smiled. Happy together. And Samantha was smiling at Luis in a way she would never smile at him, in a way no girl might ever smile at him.

Paolo turned away. Why should he care? He'd go watch the whales. But somehow, this Saturday the pleasure of free hours hung heavy as a sack of coal on his shoulders.

"Paolo, get up! The sun already climbs the sky. I've packed us a breakfast. *Rápido!* Hurry, or all the birds and guanacos will have eaten and gone to cover. I'd like to sketch on the way to Whale Camp."

"Whale Camp, Papa?" Paolo sat right up in bed.

"Didn't I tell you? We're invited to help the Martins settle in their new home."

"*Bueno.*" Paolo sprang out of bed and five minutes later Papa was starting the Jeep. The *viejo* wanted to sketch ostriches or guanacos, so they headed for the meadow where Luis had spotted the herd on Friday.

"Part of the herd's back. Luis spooked them—by accident," Paolo said, opening the car door quietly. They'd parked on the rise above the meadow and walked about halfway down, stopping at a ledge. The guanacos froze and laid back their ears warily, but Paolo and Papa sat quietly, and in a few minutes the animals turned to nibbling grass.

Papa raised one eyebrow in the comical way he had. "Can you call in one of the guanacos, Son?"

Paolo imitated a guanaco's high whinny, and a half-grown male trotted over. He sniffed at the offered grass. Papa took colored pencils from his pack and set to work drawing a furry, cinnamon-colored animal with soulful brown eyes. He sketched furiously, trying to get the outline, the mouth and eyes, before the animal bolted.

"There was a newborn left alone the other day. I almost brought it home."

"Good Lord, Son! We'd never keep one of these kids out of the house—first open door—zoom—it'd

run around the room peeing on every single drawing
I had leaning against the wall—marking its territory
like any good guanaco. A year's work peed to nothing.
No thanks. Happily for us, its mother must have returned."

"I guess."

"Think I caught a likeness?" He held up a sketch
that showed a proud inquisitive face, eyes poignantly
bewildered, mainly red-brown but with patches of
tawny baby fluff.

"Magnífico."

"Good. I'll include it with sketches for Leonora.
Your mother liked guanacos."

Papa stood staring into space for a moment, then
hunched his shoulders, put his sketchpad in the pack,
and climbed slowly back up to the car.

Paolo stared after him. His voice had gone gentle
again, as if he was still in love with Mama. But five
years ago Mama'd come—laughing and dancing
around the house, looking at Papa with smiling brown
eyes. "I look at Paolo and see my eyes. He cannot deny
me," she'd said.

She and Papa were happy—for about two days.
Then Mama said maybe they should start over—in
San Francisco. And Papa said he was willing to start
over—but only in Puerto Piramides, where his life and
work were. How about her American life? Mama
asked. And the arguing began. Ugh! But maybe Papa
had forgotten how awful it was and thought sending

Paolo to San Francisco would somehow bring Mama home?

"*Hijo*, come on. The Martins are waiting," Papa called urgently.

Paolo climbed into the Jeep, wondering if he *was* being sent as a lure. It would explain a lot. They rode in silence for some time, each absorbed in his own thoughts. Engine noise and the whine of the wind made talking difficult anyhow.

The spiky bushes had burst into bloom, transforming the barren land into a pinky-blue and yellow bouquet. Spring was brief, a few days at the most, and they feasted their eyes.

But Paolo brooded. Why was Papa so determined? He *must* want her back. Why else? Education? Hadn't Papa himself said he'd learn more from watching the whales than from reading about them?

"Papa?"

"Glorious, isn't it, Son?" Then he let go of the wheel and spread his arms out to the blooming desert, nearly running them into the sand.

"Hey, take it easy. Papa, I thought you needed a guanaco sketch for your new book."

"So?"

"So, why send this one to Mama?"

"I thought you might take it with you."

Paolo stared, then shook his head slowly. No! He wasn't going to leave home to bring Mama and Papa back together. No, let Papa go himself if he wanted her back.

He saw Papa's mouth tighten. But just at that moment they reached the crest of the hill overlooking Whale Camp and the blue sea beyond. Sitting a few yards up from the beach was the little wooden shack used by visiting researchers. The shack seemed to Paolo too fragile to withstand both the windswept desert sands and the ocean. One little house standing against the elements. For the next six months it would be the Martins' home.

"It looks too lonely for Samantha," Paolo said.

"Not if she likes whales or elephant seals," Papa replied. "I don't see their car, though."

Paolo didn't either, but he did see Dr. Martin sitting on the stoop petting what looked like a lamb. As they drew closer he saw that Dr. Martin was holding a little guanaco, a kicking bleating baby.

"Good heavens, Martin, who's your friend?" asked Papa, switching off the ignition and leaping out of the Jeep.

"Not my friend. Charley's. I've told her I'm not giving two a.m. bottles to any more babies, but here I am."

He held up a baby bottle filled with milk and then tried to nurse the baby guanaco, who butted the bottle away and went on bleating. Even in jeans and a sweatshirt Samantha's father gave the impression of a man wearing a suit and tie. Maybe it was only his hair combed strand by strand over the bald spot.

"Paolo, can you take over? There's a rubber glove in the car. A glove lets you squirt milk into his mouth until he can suck," Papa explained to Samantha's father.

"I'd appreciate that, Paolo. There's so much to do, moving in, but I can't let the poor creature starve just because that lovesick kid Luis thought he'd curry favor with Samantha by bringing her sister a pet."

"More likely your whole family will end up this guanaco's pets," Papa muttered, going for the glove.

"Luis? But the herd's coming back." Luis must have ridden out yesterday after fishing, found the baby alone, and felt it was his fault. Paolo shook his head, reached out, and set the fluffy guanaco on wobbly legs, watching to see if he'd run. They looked at each other. Paolo grinned. The *chulengo* sidled up and rubbed against his thigh.

"Okay, we're friends." Quickly Paolo dipped his finger in the milk and let the calf lick his fingers while he poured milk from the bottle into the glove. Then, ever so gently, he squeezed the rubber glove finger when the *chulengo* opened its mouth. The animal looked startled. Paolo squeezed. Again. And again. Soon he was able to lift the baby guanaco onto his lap while it looked up at him out of enormous sad eyes and contentedly finished the milk in the glove.

"You're a miracle worker, Paolo. Spoonheart and I thank you so much."

"Didn't I tell you my son had a way with wild animals?"

"He's good with him, a lot better than I am, that's for sure. I'm looking forward to meeting that albino whale calf of his. Any chance of taking me out in the skiff after school one day next week, Paolo? I'd like to get my own photos of a few heads, take a look at how the callosities differ for myself."

"Sure, I'll take you. Where's Samantha, Dr. Martin? And Charley and Señora Martin?" he asked as an afterthought, pouring more milk into the glove while the furry guanaco calf, already the size of a fair-sized dog, rubbed against him, trying to nudge milk from the glove.

"Bringing another load from town. Samantha wanted her trunk of quilting materials. Hauled them all the way from San Francisco. Has this idea of quilting a square for everything she wants to remember, a diary quilt she calls it. Well, poor kid, she had to give up her swimming—Junior Olympic trials. Anyhow, they'll be along any minute because she knows you're coming."

"Anything I can do to help?" Papa asked.

After the two men went inside the house, Paolo lifted the guanaco onto his lap and sang softly. It lay quietly in his arms, drinking a second glove of milk.

"So, Spoonheart, you'll be Charley's friend and she'll feed you and protect you from foxes and the poachers who would skin you and leave you for the vultures. You'll live by the edge of the sea and play with the seals and the penguins. And when Luis comes and says, 'See what I brought just for you, Samantha'—spit, spit straight in his eye!"

At that moment, as if on cue, Paolo saw the Martins' red Jeep head out of a ball of dust and come rattling down the hill toward them. The guanaco saw the car too and, laying back his ears, gave a high, whinnying laugh. Then he jumped out of Paolo's arms and scooted around the corner of the house, out of sight, just as the Jeep pulled to a screeching stop.

"Gordo, great, you did come. What happened? You look like somebody's socked you," Samantha said, tumbling out of the car.

"Fell. Nothing, really."

Samantha gave him one of her looks but said nothing.

"Where's Spoonheart? I saw him! Oooooh, give it here, let me have that glove," Charley cried, running over. "Spoonheart hates me," she added, her freckled face sad.

Paolo saw the guanaco peering around the corner of the house. "I've fed him with the glove, but I'll show you how later."

"I'd hate you too if I was weak from hunger and

you were always chasing me," Samantha said, ruffling Charley's red hair.

"He likes you better than me," Charley said, sniffling.

"Let *him* come to you, don't try to teach him any tricks, feed him every day, and he'll love you," Paolo promised.

"It's the one we saw. Luis brought him in to save his life," Samantha said.

"He should have waited. We went by this morning and the herd's coming back," Paolo couldn't resist saying.

"A fox could have eaten him last night," Samantha snapped.

"A fox *may* eat him if he's not protected by his herd," Paolo shot back.

6 A month later, toward the end of October, Paolo and his father were at Whale Camp having dinner with the Martins, as they now had a habit of doing on Sundays. They'd had what Señora Martin called a "standing invitation" ever since the day Paolo taught the guanaco, Spoonheart, to drink milk. Dr. Martin said they needed a consultant to help them cope with the worst baby in the family.

Today Paolo wanted badly to show Samantha Mama's letter, but so far, he hadn't been able to get her alone. All along Papa claimed he was sending Paolo to San Francisco because Mama wanted to know her son. Well, she didn't know why Papa was doing this any more than he did!

He watched Samantha setting out coffee and cookies. She was smiling at Papa, who was going on and on about how he and Paolo went swimming with the whales this morning. Making it sound like they were the greatest friends in the world. Actually, since he told Papa he wasn't going north and Papa said his decision to send Paolo away to school was final, not open to discussion, they hardly talked at all.

"But the really amazing thing, almost eerie," Papa was saying, "is that every week but one, this albino calf and his mother come racing over. And the calf puts on a breaching and splashing show just for us, right, Son?"

"I'd rather swim more and watch less," Paolo said.

"When they get to playing, they forget their own strength and we could find ourselves in real trouble. Looks like you've got friends, though, Son."

Paolo hated the sweet talking Papa did in public these days. He did like being with the Martins, though. Until he was eight and saw Mama and Papa arguing, he used to dream she'd come back and make *them* a family. A kid's dream.

The Martins were the first real—two-parent—family he'd ever known well. You never knew what was coming next in their conversation. Their laughter was like background music. Later, at home, he'd hear their laughter again, echoing through his silent room, far off and loving, like families on television.

However, tonight he desperately wanted to talk to Samantha alone, and he'd spent two hours trying to coax her out of the house. Her turn to cook dinner, she said.

"Strong? He butts me right over twenty times a

day," Charley said, managing to bring the conversation back to her guanaco once again.

"Maybe he thinks he's a goat," Paolo said, looking toward the front door and then back to Samantha, who shook her head.

"He's never seen a goat. He thinks he's a Martin—he tries to use the bathroom but doesn't understand about toilets—another kid in toilet training, Mom says."

"Tell everything, Samantha," Charley snapped.

"I think it's flattering that he tries to copy us."

"Sure. Daddy doesn't blame you when he messes."

Samantha was passing coffee and only shrugged.

"Paolo, what do you think?"

"Probably instinct. Guanaco herds use communal dung heaps in the wild."

"You can't train him out of instinct, Charley," added Papa.

"Paolo! Stop looking at Samantha when you're talking to me. Stop it!"

"Was I, Charley? Sorry." He blushed and lowered his eyes.

"You've been staring at her all night. Finish eating so Spoonheart can come back in."

Paolo blushed even more and handed over his plate. Señora Martin put the guanaco outside while they ate because with his long neck, he could reach the center of the table and sweep off food and the plates, glasses, and silverware as well. He was already the size of a colt, and it was fun watching him stalk around the room.

Samantha and Charley were clearing the table as if in a speeded-up old Charlie Chaplin movie while Spoonheart whinnied and scratched at the door.

"Okay, Mom?"

"Get that butter and the place mats, Samantha. Grab your wineglasses and coffee mugs, everybody. All right, baby, let the monster in."

"Freezing out, Mom," Charley said, heading for the door.

"That's why he's got fur," said Dr. Martin.

Charley opened the door to a blast of wind and Spoonheart stampeded past her. She tried to grab him, but he butted her so hard she fell backward and he kept going.

"Close that door," said Dr. Martin.

"Sure hope he makes it this time," said Samantha, grabbing a dustpan and the mop. "Oh, darn, he missed. He's peeing in the doorway again. Come help me, Gordo."

Paolo arrived in time to see the guanaco braced against the corner of the bathroom, squirting urine and pellets all over the floor. On his face was a look of human relief.

"Figures," said Paolo. "Guanacos use herd dung heaps and Spoonheart's part of this family, isn't he?"

"You said that before. Like Luis says, you have to

know everything. Here, dump this on Mom's garden, genius," Samantha said, handing him a dustpan full of pellets.

"Come with me."

"In a few minutes."

Spoonheart trotted alongside, sniffing at the pellets, nuzzling Paolo, until he reached the front door. Then he backed off, obviously afraid of being put outside again. Paolo braved the wind and dumped the pellets in Señora Martin's petunia bed. Luis *always* said he had to know everything, but Samantha saying it too— that hurt. It was probably a mistake to tell her about the letter until she was in a better mood, but he had to know what she'd think.

He waited outside, listening to the night herons flying up into the dusk, each with one triumphant cry, night fishers, at home in the darkening sky and surf.

Suddenly the door opened and she was there, wrapped in a windbreaker, her legs bare against the wind, blond hair whipping her face, so beautiful he inhaled deeply, whistling a little. *"Hola,"* he said.

"Sorry, Gordo."

He nodded, looking into her blue eyes. "Princess Samantha."

"What's up?"

His expression fell.

"So?"

"My father left a letter lying open—from my mother—and I read it."

"And you're furiously hurt. What does she say?"

"She says, 'I wonder whatever possessed you to think of sending Paolo to me now, at this vulnerable point in his life. His education, I suppose, but knowing you, this idea probably hit *him* like a bolt of lightning. We're strangers. The poor kid must be devastated—booted out by Papa and shipped across the seas to a mama he hasn't seen in five years. Away from the peninsula you've trained him to love above anyplace on earth.' " Paolo looked at Samantha, shaking his head slightly.

"She knows how you feel. So you've memorized it. And?"

"So Papa's dumping me. He *said* she wanted me, and this proves that's a lie. Like she says, we're strangers. I think Papa wants Mama back."

"And he's using you as bait? Could be. Well, come on to S.F. and live with us. We all like you—a lot."

"Samantha—that's not the point!"

"It could be. Let's go in. I'm freezing."

"He's my *father*."

Samantha shrugged. "Right, and even I can see how much he loves you, Gordo. Did she say she didn't want you?"

"No."

"Then this can wait till tomorrow. I'm freezing. Goose pimples, see?"

"I thought we were friends, Samantha."

"Why else would I come out in this blizzard?"

They opened the door to hear Charley sobbing. Dr. Martin had his arms around her. Samantha ignored Charley, picked up her quilting, and sat down at the far table with Señora Martin and Paolo's father.

"What's wrong?" Paolo asked.

"Spoonheart spit at me. He ha-a-ates me," Charley said, gulping back sobs.

"He doesn't like you to hug him. Let him nuzzle you."

"Bad Spoonheart!"

"Charley, he thinks you're a baby like him and he wants to be the alpha wolf," Samantha said, biting off her thread.

"Mom, Samantha thinks I'm a baby."

"Well, you're acting like one, dear."

Paolo walked over to join those at the table. Samantha's words stung. But she was cold. She *did* have goose pimples. And she *did* invite him to live with them. Not that he would. He watched her fingers embroidering tiny red stitches into the outline of a crab so real you could almost see the claws move. Spoonheart settled down quietly at his feet. There was a moment's silence.

"Were you talking about me?" Paolo asked Papa finally, with an edge to his voice.

"As a matter of fact, yes."

"Your father was telling us you'll be coming to San Francisco for school next year," Señora Martin said. "We're thrilled."

Paolo frowned at his father. "I'd rather see you here, Señora."

"But we'll be leaving."

"I'd like to go abroad to school, once in my life," Samantha said.

"You are, remember?"

"*Without family*. Frankly, Dr. Alvarez," Samantha continued, turning to Papa, "if you send Gordo into the city without me to protect him, I'd be afraid he'd get run over, squashed like those tuco-tuco rats you see on the roads."

"I'm sending him so he'll learn enough not to be squashed, Samantha. So he'll be comfortable out in the world."

"Sink or swim, huh?"

Papa and Samantha thought they were so smart, talking as if he wasn't there, as if he hadn't refused to go, as if his going was settled. As if Papa were deaf to his saying no. And what would happen to Spoonheart, asleep at his feet, when Samantha and her family left? "Doesn't anyone ever get to stay anyplace—ever?" he asked in a sad voice.

"Oh, Son," groaned Papa.

"I felt that way—as you continually remind me, Gordo—and now I feel we've lived here forever and you're my best friend." Samantha began cutting out a paper pattern of a whale for another quilting square. White Calf on a blue background. Her Peninsula Valdes quilt diary for her friends at home. Her blond hair shone in the lamplight, and she smiled as she stitched.

"You'll have another best friend next year, Samantha." And another boyfriend, he thought.

"So will you."

Paolo knew better, but he didn't reply. They'd just say, Sure you will. Instead he did his disappearing act. He stayed in his chair but shifted his mind away, away from them all, back to the night herons outside. There were no trees around here, so where did herons sleep during the day?

He felt a weight and found Charley leaning against his shoulder, just for a moment, before she slid down to the floor and curled up next to the sleeping guanaco, gingerly, careful not to wake him, and closed her eyes. Poor Charley. He could have found her a dog if Luis hadn't rushed to the rescue like gangbusters.

"Well, Son," Papa said, standing up. "Time to go. Ornithologists have to watch the early bird, you know, especially since we took off and went swimming today."

"You say that every time, Dr. Alvarez."

"To hear your chuckle, Samantha. It's a rare girl who can chuckle."

"Want to go swimming after school tomorrow, Samantha?" Maybe if they were alone, he could make her understand.

"With the whales?"

"Indeed not, young lady," said Señora Martin.

"When, then? I was the best backstroke in the city."

"Perhaps your daughter could come out in the boat with Paolo and me sometime?"

"That's kind of you, Raul. We'll see," replied Señora Martin in a very cool voice.

Samantha sighed. "Okay, I'll go swimming tomorrow if you help me gather shells for my class in San Francisco, Gordo."

Then there was the usual flurry of good-byes. After they were out in the Jeep, their headlights the only beacon in the moonless night, Paolo turned and looked back at those lighted windows in the beach shack.

So solitary. So fragile against the immensity of cliffs and sea and desert. Only the Martins for thirty miles in any direction. Only the Martins and the whales and elephant seals they'd come halfway around the world to study. No wonder Charley kept trying to hug a guanaco who butted and spit at her. No wonder Samantha needed him for a best friend *and* Luis for a boyfriend.

"Papa?"

"Hm?"

"Charley's like me. She doesn't belong in a new place—so she pesters Spoonheart."

His father was hunched over the wheel, peering into the night ahead, and didn't answer. Concentrating. This was a dangerous stretch. Animals crossed the road, walked along it, lay down and slept on it, even mated on the road here.

Finally Papa cleared his throat. "Don't you trust yourself to cross a street without Samantha?"

"It's Samantha who's always thinking of a million other things and needs help crossing, not me."

Papa laughed easily. "Anyhow, Luis will be dropping out in December. We can't expect the school to run a class just for you after Samantha goes," he said.

"Why would Luis drop out?"

"He told Señora Martin it's too hard to work and keep up with school. His mama's not well. I thought you knew."

"Quit school—after eighth grade? But how's he going to be an engineer?" The day he'd socked him, Luis had said Paolo didn't know *anything* about his life. Did he mean having to quit school?

"But you don't know my life either, Luis," Paolo whispered. A year ago he and Luis would have read the letter from Mama together, figured how to keep Luis in school and Paolo at home. Now Luis was dropping out and everyone assumed Paolo could be shipped off to San Francisco. To a stranger. "Papa, Mama never asked for me," he said quietly.

"You took my letter, didn't you? Should be ashamed, reading my mail. She wants you, Son, that's only her way of getting a little jab at me. If it was just Leonora or school or even just how solitary your life is here—but—please trust me, Son. I went away to school. It's time for you to see the world. And Mama wants you. It's best. And now let me pay attention to this road or we'll never make it home."

So the subject was closed, as usual. Not this time. "Well," Paolo said slowly, "you'll have to kidnap me to make me go."

THE FIGHT

7 "So did your papa say he's going to kidnap you?" Samantha asked as they climbed down the rocky path to Pampano Beach the next afternoon.

"He said we seem to be stalemated. That's all." Summer already, Paolo thought as warm wind brushed his face. Only two more months and the whales would leave. White Calf and his mother would swim out the channel and disappear into the sea. Three months and the new school term would start in San Francisco. Well, he'd said it. Papa would have to kidnap him to send him to Mama.

"So he knows you're desperate. That'll give him second thoughts. Oh, don't you love the wind when it's warm?"

Paolo smiled. He loved the solitude here and the way the sea lions swam close inshore and then hauled themselves out onto the beach to sleep under the summer sun. He loved looking out over the water to the birds and the whale blows. "You do like it here."

"Look at all these shells—I could set up shop," called Samantha, wading into them.

"You wouldn't find many customers. Not when every tide throws up more." They could fill a gunnysack for her friends in ten minutes and be done. "The only shell I keep is a conch—my private ocean to lull me to sleep."

"Shell heaven. The ones they sell in San Francisco probably come from here."

"Luis and I used to come for the shells his mother put in her paintings. Sometimes she'd even let us help with the paintings." A mistake to mention Luis, but he'd been thinking of him, of asking him to go out— swimming with the whales. He'd wanted to ask today, but Luis wasn't at school. He was absent a lot these days and glum when he did show up.

"Oh, Gordo, all these divine shells. And those black-and-white birds swimming. Don't tell me they're—"

"Penguins. The penguins are back! In another week you'll see millions." Half a dozen penguins waddled ashore, clapping wings against their bodies to dry off.

"Like they're wearing tuxedos." Samantha sighed.

"Never heard a tourist who didn't say that."

"Soooo? I'm a tourist and so what? Now I can make a penguin patch for my quilt!"

Paolo pointed out a harem of sea lions far down the beach, and as he did so he noticed the solitary figure walking toward them. He knew Luis by his curious loping gait, though apparently Samantha hadn't seen him yet. They could still leave and have the afternoon to themselves. But maybe Luis could swim with the whales tomorrow? And if they could find a way to keep Luis in school next year, maybe Papa would relent? "Luis!"

Then Samantha started waving, both hands high over her head. And Luis waved back. Paolo watched him coming, trying to gauge his mood. Not too good.

"So—Samantha—you were coming home to meet my mother today and I find you with Gordo instead?" Luis stood before them, frowning, legs planted wide, hands on hips.

"No! You said you'd tell me today because sometimes she's too sick. And you weren't in school, so I thought, his mama, she had a bad day."

"*Hola*, Luis," Paolo said.

"My mother made *flan* for you, Samantha."

"I'm sorry, but how was I to know? How about tomorrow? If you're well enough to come to school."

"I'm not sick."

"Then if she wasn't worse and you weren't sick, where were you?"

"*Hola*, Luis."

"I see you, Gordo. Samantha stood me up."

"I most certainly did not! You stood my mother up by not coming to school. How do you think that makes me feel?"

"My mother got out of bed and made custard for you."

"So, next time tell me!"

"I washed the windows for you."

"They'll still be clean tomorrow."

"Let's go swimming," Paolo said.

"In a minute."

"Luis, do you hear a word I'm saying? My mother is your teacher."

"Only married women nag their men, *querida.*"

Samantha stripped to her bathing suit without another word and ran for the water. Paolo watched her pull off blouse and shorts, toss them and run until the cold surf lapped around her ankles. She stood tall for a moment, hesitating; her body quivered a little in a pink bikini almost the color of her skin. He knew he was staring, saw Luis looking too and hated that. The two boys watched in silence as she waded out into the quiet water and dove in. She swam out beyond the breakers, straight into deep water, with a strong, sure stroke. Then she turned over and paralleled the beach, backstroking, as if she were swimming laps.

"Did you know she swims every day—she's a champion," Paolo said.

"Of course," Luis said with a raised eyebrow.

"Let's go swimming."

"Didn't I tell you to stay away from her?"

Paolo felt the tightness in his stomach that edgy tone always brought. He looked up, but Luis was still watching Samantha, who'd come back into the surf close to shore, followed by two penguins.

"First penguins she's ever seen," Paolo said, to make Luis look away from her.

"Yeah?" Luis said, without looking away. Then he turned a perfect handspring and ran off toward the water, still in his jean cutoffs. They'd been Paolo's cutoffs but they got too tight around the hips. Never looked good on him, but they fit Luis like custom-made. No hips.

Paolo heard Samantha call for Luis to come on in; the water, she said, was fine. Luis blew Samantha a kiss and dove in, surfacing near her. They were laughing. They'd forgotten visiting his mother, forgotten *him*. They acted as if he didn't exist—just another fat sea lion sunning himself. Maybe he'd just go on home. Let Luis help her pick up shells for her stupid class.

"Hey, Gordo, come on in. The water's warm."

"I'm coming, Samantha." She hadn't forgotten him, after all. Feeling their eyes on him, Paolo jogged out to the water and dove in. Once in the water, though, he felt good, graceful and at ease.

After their swim Samantha wanted to collect shells and watch the sea lion harem, so all three started down the beach. For a few minutes it was great. They started turning handsprings, then marking out a big hopscotch on the sand, each picking a shell for their marker. Samantha chose a sand dollar.

It was hard to say exactly how the trouble started, how the mood changed. Maybe it started when Luis put his arm around Samantha's shoulders to congratulate her on a good hopscotch throw. Paolo didn't like it, but Samantha laughed and said thanks.

Next time she made a good toss, Luis tried to kiss her. Samantha turned her head away. "No."

"Since when?"

"You know."

"Him?"

"No. Since you've stopped coming to school."

"Your mother knows I need to leave school. Maybe I have to take my mother to the doctor. Maybe work, always something."

"I miss you," Samantha said softly.

"Maybe I'll quit school too, end of eighth. I won't have to leave home that way," Paolo interrupted.

"What could you do?" Luis asked curiously.

Paolo shrugged. "I'd make a good tour guide. But if you stayed in school, maybe they'd give us a class and we'd both be better off."

"For me, impossible. For you, with a papa with all the money in the world to send his boy to San Francisco, California, why not go? Gordo, can't you understand? I don't choose to work. I have to work."

"You worked and went to school this year," Paolo said.

"And I was stupid tired both places." Luis shook his head, and for a moment, Paolo saw sheer misery in his face. Then his mouth hardened, eyes turning black, like obsidian. "Your mother won't take you, eh?"

"You know I belong here."

"We asked him to live with us," Samantha said quietly.

"No! Luis, I'm not going to, so don't be jealous."

"Me? Jealous? Grow up, Gordo! Anyhow, you don't know one thing about Samantha and me." Suddenly Luis exploded. "Go on home, nature boy!"

"Stay, Gordo!" Samantha said.

"Get out of here!"

"Stay!"

"Get out!" Luis took a step toward him, his face turning wild.

Paolo stood there, deciding, the surf behind them, a steep climb to the road in front. Sometimes he could outrun Luis. But *she'd* never leave, and he couldn't leave her here alone. He was in for it this time.

"Big bully. You disgust me," Samantha said.

Luis shrugged. "So? You break dates. Flirt."

For a moment they all hesitated. And it was Paolo who broke the spell. "Let's all go. Your mothers will both be waiting," he said.

And when Samantha silently kneeled in the sand to pick up her bag of shells, Paolo sighed. It would be all right, after all.

But then Luis reached for her, his hand tightening on her arm. "Samantha?"

"Let go of me, you *macho* brute," she whispered.

"Hey, take your hands off her!" Paolo yelled, surprising himself.

Luis let go of Samantha and came straight for Paolo. He socked him in the stomach, followed with an uppercut to the chin.

Paolo was stunned, then humiliated. Samantha was seeing this! Enough was enough!

Then he got mad, madder than he'd ever been. He saw red, literally a flash of red, and he brought his fist down on Luis's black head of hair while he was still crouched down, ready to strike again. He'd never hit Luis before, and it felt good. And once started he just kept punching away, not knowing where he was hitting or what he was doing, really, just punching into that hard body and feeling it give, rumble, crack. The more he hit that body, the more he wanted to.

And each time he punched him, Luis muttered or went "oof" or yelled, and this was deeply satisfying. Far away in the background Samantha screamed. And Paolo knew that Luis was socking him too, and he felt his blood running off his arm and face, but it didn't matter. Even the pain didn't matter anymore. "How do you like it? Huh? Huh?"

"Okay, okay, *bueno,* enough," Luis kept saying, forcing the words in pained grunts.

"Help, help! They're killing each other!"Paolo heard Samantha calling.

And her voice carried the shrillness of gulls before a storm. And he was pleased. Good! She said they were killing *each other.* Luis must be hurt too. He could fight back. At last. At last. Samantha had seen that he could fight back.

"Can't take it, huh!" he grunted between blows.

"All right!"

Then suddenly Paolo felt a blinding pain, a knee in his groin, and he doubled over and then, somehow, fell backward and hit his head on a rock outcropping. He felt himself fall, heard his head crack sharply, and had time to think Luis had finally killed him—though the pain in his groin was too excruciating for him to care. Then darkness took away the pain, not all at once, but he spiraled slowly down and down into an emptiness, gray, and green, and, finally, black.

RECOVERY

8 Paolo awoke in the dark, pitch-black wherever he looked. He tried to turn his head, but the pain was too great. Had he gone blind then—not died but broken his head open? He remembered hitting his head. He remembered a knee in the groin—he moved his legs and felt better down there. And then he discovered the moon and found he could still see, after all. Stars. A window. A white wall—the only white walls in town were at the medical clinic. There was another bed in the room and someone asleep, snoring lightly. Papa's snore. Papa was here with him. He smiled and closed his eyes. He could feel the light without opening his eyes.

Then he woke to the morning. Sunlight. Papa, Samantha, Luis, the doctor, and a nurse all stood around his bed, bumping into one another. "Where's the party?" he asked.

"Right here with you, Son," Papa said.

"How do you feel, young man?" asked Dr. Oliva.

"My head hurts if I move."

"I should think so." The doctor nodded and squeezed his shoulder.

Paolo turned a little toward Luis. "*Hola*, Luis."

"I was afraid I'd killed you."

"Not your fault you didn't," Papa said.

Paolo tried to shake his head, but the pain was too great. "I fought too," he said, seeing Luis's eye swollen shut and ugly bruises up one side of his face.

"Like a tiger," Luis said.

"You really cracked yourself one." Dr. Oliva, who played chess with Papa on Tuesday nights, was peering into his eyes with a flashlight. Samantha said nothing. He wanted to hear her voice, but it hurt too much to turn his head enough to look at her.

"Hi, Samantha," he said.

All day he kept waking up and then drifting back to sleep. Sometimes the doctor or Papa would wake him and give him juice or water to drink with a straw. Sometimes Samantha was there, sometimes Luis.

Once he heard Samantha and Luis arguing in the hall when his door had been left open.

"I told you—it's no good. You could have killed Gordo."

"Yes, I know. I feel so bad, never so bad before."

"Sure, until the next time."

"I said no. No more."

"Next time Gordo will beat you to a pulp, would have yesterday if you fought fair."

"You want us fighting over you again, is that it?"

"No. Luis, no. I know you were friends until I came."

"No, you're a flirt, but even before you came, I hated it that Gordo had it so easy, a father, always enough money. He never saw that I had it harder, either. Then when Mama couldn't work—only me—"

"Listen! Dad and I had a long talk yesterday. I did tease you both. You never would have fought if I hadn't—"

Paolo tried to call, but his voice came out a whisper. Then Samantha's voice grew gentle, Luis's too soft to hear clearly. They must have moved farther down the hall. Had he been fighting over Samantha? One minute they were hopscotching on wet sand and then they'd been socking each other, but he couldn't remember why, exactly. Only the satisfying blows. Only fighting back.

"You're growing up, Paolo," said the doctor a day or two later. "Wouldn't surprise me if you end up tall and skinny like your mama. You've got her rosy cheeks and romantic eyes, too."

Tall and skinny! The words kept repeating in Paolo's head like the litany in church and he didn't know if he was dreaming or if the doctor had actually said them. He didn't always know when he was dreaming these last days.

*   *   *

"I'm hungry," he said at last. The fuzziness was gone and he was sitting up. Samantha was standing by his bed, and she laughed. It hurt that she laughed. "I haven't eaten all day, have I?"

"Nor yesterday. Nor the day before. It's about time you showed some appetite. Hold on. Your father's bringing ice cream."

"Chocolate?"

"I'm sorry, Gordo. I—I mean, you and Luis were friends and then I came—and the fight—it all happened so fast. And I thought I'd lie down and die when I heard your head crack on that rock. That second I knew how much you mean to me, how I love you," Samantha said, and then quickly changed the subject. "By the way, I'm embroidering a square with your bandaged head for the quilt. And Mama had everyone in the school write you a letter today."

"They'll all hate me because they had to write letters." Had she really said she loved him? But before he could ask, Papa appeared with the ice cream.

"Hope you all like chocolate," he said.

Later that night—or was it the next night?—Luis slipped into the room alone. He stood by the bed, shifting from one foot to the other, spurs jangling.

Paolo felt uneasy. He wasn't afraid. Not anymore. But there was something else. He'd liked hitting Luis, and he felt a little sick thinking about it. He'd liked hitting his best friend. He felt his face flush.

"He hates me, your papa—says I tried to kill you. It's not true, but I have this bad temper. You fight well."

"Forget it." Paolo blushed at the praise.

Luis shook his head, and his eyes were moist. "Samantha says I have to say the bad things out loud so they won't happen again. The priest, he says I am in the sin of jealousy. You have a papa, money, the smartest head in class, and now you can go to school in Norte América. You don't know what that would mean to the rest of us. A chance!

"Even the wild animals come running or flying or swimming when you call, Gordo. Me, I wear your old clothes. Mama cleans the school, and now she's too sick and I earn our food, her medicines. But when the whales leave, there's no tourists. No work, no money. What will we do then?"

Paolo was quiet. He couldn't remember Luis saying so much about himself ever before. What could he say? "But my clothes always look better on you."

Luis laughed then as Paolo hoped he would and straightened his shoulders a little. "Well, maybe. But you're growing like a weed."

Suddenly Paolo remembered his plan. "But Luis, engineers always find work. If you stay in school—"

"If I stay in school, Mama and I will starve before the New Year."

"Not if you get your mama's job cleaning the school."

Luis shook his head. "Don't talk craziness; that

hardly buys bread. And if I stay in school, it won't help you. Your papa wants you away from me, from here, to see the world."

"It's worth trying. A chance, for both of us. And you could stay in school. Please, Luis."

He saw Luis's mouth tighten then and his fists clench and unclench at his sides. Temper, temper, as Samantha said. Let Luis think it over. Paolo waited a moment and then spoke to break the silence.

"Your mother, what's wrong?" Paolo's words surprised himself because he hadn't been thinking of Luis's mother, a wild woman who had chased him out of the school with a broom while she cleaned. She even pinched sometimes.

"The *médicos*, they don't say. She called the lawyer and had a paper made, putting the house in my name—because she doubts—about living much longer."

"You own a house!"

"That's what the lawyer says."

"But that's a *maravilla*. I didn't know a boy *could* own a house. She really must trust you."

"She wants me to have someplace to live—after."

Paolo's excitement drained as he looked at Luis and saw the pain in his eyes. Why, Luis loved that crazy woman who yelled at everybody—he loved her—his mama. Like he loved Papa. Luis had no father, no one else. If his mama died, he'd be alone in his house. Without anyone even to talk to. "Maybe she'll get well, after all," he said, and his words didn't seem right, not enough. "I sure hope so," he added.

Luis looked surprised, then shrugged and spread wide his hands. "If God wishes," he said. Then he started pacing the floor. "I'd better go. Take care."

At that moment Papa and Samantha came in, Samantha carrying a tray covered with a white napkin. Papa went straight to Luis. "I told you to stay away."

"I had something I had to tell Gordo—sir."

"You damn near kill him and then you chat?"

"It was so. See you later, Gordo. I told him, Samantha," said Luis, letting himself out the door.

"All of it?" Samantha asked, but he was gone.

"Luis—don't forget—let's go swim with the whales," Paolo called after him.

"Take me too," Samantha said.

Papa groaned.

"Suppose I'd cracked Luis's head on that rock, Papa?"

"Son, you think I don't know who started that fight?"

"Anyway, Luis's mother signed over their house to him. She must really love him to do that, no?" Paolo wasn't about to discuss the fight in front of Samantha!

"They say she's really ill," Papa said.

"Mom told me she has cancer," Samantha added.

"Poor soul. By the way, I've got some good news."

"Dr. Alvarez! You promised I could tell him."

"Samantha! Forgive me."

"You can go home tomorrow, Gordo!" Samantha laughed and clapped.

Home. Home with Papa. "My own room. You're not kidding? Can I get up? Go back to school?"

"The doctor says another week or two."

"I brought your homework," Samantha said, dumping papers out of her shoulder bag onto the bed. "Charley drew you a picture of Spoonheart, but the brute peed all over it."

"Shows what he thinks of Charley's drawing."

"Shows she can't draw on the floor with a guanaco in the house. Dad says Spoonheart's going to drive us out of house and home. It's him or us."

Later that night, Paolo was thinking over Luis's strange visit. Strange because, for one thing, Luis talked more than he had in years and hadn't mentioned Samantha. Samantha looked straight at Luis when she came in this afternoon and he wouldn't even look back. Maybe they'd been breaking up when he heard them arguing? And what *had* Luis meant the day of the fight—that Paolo didn't know anything about him and Samantha? What was there to know? What had Samantha meant when she said she loved *him*? His pulse raced.

It started raining, and he lay awake listening to the patterns of raindrops hitting the tin roof. Maybe the doctor wouldn't let him go home in a storm? Or Papa would be afraid and wouldn't take him? It only rained three or four days all year on the peninsula, so why now?

Sometime during the night the storm passed, and Paolo woke to find his bed bathed in sunlight. Late that afternoon Papa came to take him home. As Paolo climbed into the Jeep he asked the question he'd been going over in his mind all day.

"Papa, could we drive over to a beach so I could see the bay? Only a few minutes. I just want to see the birds—maybe a whale—it's been so long."

"A week. But I suppose, for a boy who's trying to keep track of a certain albino whale, that's a long while. You'll stay in the car?"

He promised, and they drove to the beach where their boat was tied. It seemed as if he'd forgotten how sky and water blended, enveloping the tawny sand. Far down the beach sea lions lay in the sun. Out on the bay birds fought over a school of fish and a whale spouted. Then half a dozen more. Paolo was happy. White Calf was out there somewhere. He watched his father walk down toward the water.

Then he caught sight of a flash of pink where the beach gave way to sand dunes and saw Luis, and Samantha in the pink shirt she wore over her bikini, each with an arm around the other's waist. Samantha leaning her head on Luis's shoulder, looking up at him with that loving smile, a smile Paolo would never see. It was the smile that got to him, even before Samantha raised her head and Luis bent down and kissed her, kissed her as if it was his natural right, as if he'd been kissing her all their lives.

Obviously they hadn't broken up! He'd fought for her, nearly been killed—by Luis. With tears in her eyes she'd told him she loved him—and here she was out with Luis. And Luis? Some friend!

Then Samantha said something and Luis laughed. Then he kissed her lips, her neck, her lips again, holding her so close they seemed like one body. Paolo was held, spellbound. He'd never seen—didn't know—a flush spread through his entire body and he couldn't seem to swallow.

Finally they broke apart and in another moment they'd disappeared behind the dunes, leaving an emptiness in the day. But he'd seen them, and he knew nothing between the three of them would ever be the same again. It was as if they'd moved away from— what? Paolo wasn't sure except about one thing. He was the one who'd been left behind. And what's more, Samantha was a liar!

"You're right, Son. We live in beauty. I don't see your whale, though."

Papa had came back, but he hadn't noticed Luis and Samantha. He'd tell the Martins if he saw them and there'd be trouble. "Papa, let's go home. I feel funny— a little dizzy. I've had enough for one day."

9 The memory of Luis and Samantha on the beach haunted Paolo. In the days before returning to school he thought about them constantly. After all, she'd *said* she loved *him*! With tears in her eyes. How could she let Luis kiss her as she did?

So what? You knew they were going together, he'd remind himself. Well, but that was before the fight. So you thought things were different? That Samantha blamed Luis when you don't? Well, seeing them like that hurt. Was that love? Was Papa thinking about *that* when he said Leonora in such a gentle voice? He'd keep arguing with himself until he'd get a headache and give it up for the day.

And at night he dreamed about Samantha, dreamed she was in the pink bikini, running after him down the beach, and though he wanted her to catch up, he couldn't slow down. And after school, when he'd hear her footsteps on the veranda, his throat would close up and he'd rush to the door smiling, only to find her with Luis. If only she'd come alone. Or even if Luis would come by himself. But no.

"You can stay an hour. Paolo still gets headaches from too much company after such a nasty blow," Papa would say, looking straight at Luis.

Then Samantha sat on one side of his bed and Luis on the other and they'd smile at each other across him. After a while, he'd glance at his watch. Or close his eyes. Didn't matter. Neither of them left until Papa told them it was time to vamoose.

"We're the three musketeers now. We're all friends, no jealousy and no fighting. Right?" Samantha laid down the rules the first afternoon they visited.

Luis had agreed and Paolo had too. If he didn't, Paolo'd have to admit he'd seen them kissing on the beach. Which probably would have cleared the air, but he wasn't ready to hear what Samantha might say to that. Luis would say, So what? Why pretend? We're still friends.

And Luis would be right in a way. They *were* friends since the fight if only Paolo could get over his obsession with seeing Luis and Samantha together. Even so, this didn't solve any problems. They hadn't figured any way to keep Luis from quitting school or losing his job on the tourist boat, had they? Papa still thought he was sending Paolo to Mama in San Francisco, didn't he? So nothing had changed. After the fight, after all they'd said, their lives should have gotten better.

After two weeks at home, Paolo went back to school. There they sat, the three of them, knocking knees

around the eighth-grade table for six endless hours.
Samantha sat in the middle, looking from him to Luis,
fluttering those incredible eyelashes. And Luis, eager
to make Samantha think he'd changed his spots after
the fight, kept pestering them to go swimming with
the whales or, if Samantha's mother still wouldn't let
her, then horseback riding. The three of them. Always
the three of them.

When Señora Martin asked Samantha to help Paolo
catch up with homework, he thought, Great, alone at
last.

"Luis is behind too. Could I tutor them together,
Mom?"

"Good thinking, dear," said Señora Martin.

And Paolo *had* to keep Luis in school to have any
chance of staying home himself! So all he could do
was keep his big mouth shut and hate it.

Then one afternon, something snapped. They were
walking home from school. Samantha was in the habit
of staying at Paolo's house until Señora Martin picked
her up on their way back to Whale Camp, and it was
the only time Paolo had a chance of being alone with
her. Luis usually worked or had to care for his mother,
so Paolo was waiting for him to cut off down toward
the *casita*.

Instead, when they came to the cutoff, Luis put his
arms around Samantha and gave her a long passionate
kiss, right there on the road.

"Hey, cut it out. You think I'm the invisible man?"

"Only saying good-bye to my woman. Took your advice, Gordo, and I've got Mama's job—I'm the janitor this afternoon," Luis said, and walked off, grinning.

Samantha and Paolo stood looking after him a long while. Only after he disappeared into the *casita* did they continue walking.

"I didn't want that to happen, you know," Samantha said once they were on Paolo's porch.

"Luis was staking his territory."

"I'm nobody's territory and he broke our three-musketeer pact."

"But he's your boyfriend and he wanted it out in the open. Luis and me, we like our friendships honest."

"Luis has nothing to do with our friendship. Nothing."

"Spare me the details." Paolo looked around for an escape. Samantha liked to talk things out, but he didn't!

"Are you jealous?"

"Maybe I just like things honest. Luis does too."

She reached out and took his hands in hers and Paolo yanked them away. "Hey, cut that out!"

"Only being friendly. Look, Gordo, I'm trying. I don't know what to do either. Luis and I are . . . I mean, I don't know, I don't know."

"See you," Paolo said, opening the door and edging

in, but Samantha put her foot inside so he couldn't close it.

"No, you don't, buster. Either you stay right here or I'm coming in and I don't care what your father hears."

Paolo could see she meant it, so he backed out on the veranda again and, closing the door, crossed his arms against his chest. He saw her blue eyes flashing—the wind whipping her dress against her slender body, against her breasts. If only he could erase that memory of her and Luis on the beach and just be friends again. "Look, Samantha, I live here too. So?"

"But you're younger."

"You mean next year I'll understand?"

"I hope so," Samantha said icily. "Okay, I said I'm sorry about the kiss. But Luis and I only have this summer. You and I—we're friends, your mother lives in my hometown, we'll visit, write, everything—for years. The American half-breed and the Argentine half-breed. Right?"

"So why drag me along with Luis? How do you think I feel?"

"Because I like to be with you! Luis does too. Luis'd give anything to be you, you know. Going abroad instead of quitting school, an adoring papa instead of a dying mama—"

"Do you love him?"

"My feelings are none of your business, Gordo. Or are they?" Samantha fell silent, watching him closely.

"Do you love him?" He wanted to tell her about seeing them on the beach but hesitated. Did he want to hear any more?

"It's none of your business—or is it?"

Paolo stared at her. Finally he shook his head, sitting down heavily on the whale disk bench.

"So?"

"What I think is you keep me around to keep things stirred up."

Samantha turned away and shook the blond curls out of her face. Then she swung back, her face flushed, her voice angry. "*Basta!* I thought you were a friend— stupid me."

"Well, I'm not going to San Francisco, so I guess that puts me in Luis's temporary category, anyhow."

"Yes, you are."

"Wait and see."

"Don't be an idiot. If you want to save the whales and penguins and all the other folks here—you have to."

"No, I belong here, on Peninsula Valdes. I'll keep Luis from quitting school or I'll take courses by mail."

"He hasn't got time. But so what if you did? One year, big deal. What then?"

"I'd find a way. Don't worry about me!"

"Baloney. How about your mother? How about getting into a university? I thought you were intelligent."

Who was she to—Paolo couldn't take it anymore. "And I thought you were—decent!" he yelled.

Samantha stared at him for a long moment and then hauled off and slapped him hard across the face. She turned without another word and ran down the steps. "*Caramba!* Samantha. Wait!" But she was running down the road. His face stung. Let her go. Well, he deserved that slap—shouldn't have said that—wasn't what he felt—but she kept pushing and at least the three musketeers lie was over. What a relief!

And it *should* have been a relief, but he found himself listening all afternoon, expecting Samantha's voice, hoping she'd return. The house had never felt so empty, so lonely. He'd grown so used to having a soda with her after school, laughing over crazy things, talking about everything, used to looking at her. He'd never realized how good it felt to see the way a smile lit up Samantha's whole face.

Later that night, playing checkers with his father, he felt ready to explode, more like kicking the board to smithereens than concentrating on the game. So, of course, Papa had gotten two kings in the last two moves.

"I hate this game." Maybe he should get up and walk out the door. And go where? No place to go; not like he'd want to walk down the road and lay it all out on Luis like he used to. Luis never did say much, but he'd make cocoa and maybe they'd practice soccer for a while and it helped.

"Your move, Son."

"*Bueno.* Where's the fire?"

"You've got a short fuse tonight. Something wrong?"

Paolo nodded.

"Qué pasa?"

Paolo moved, careful not to leave his men vulnerable to any more jumping. He shrugged. No way he could tell Papa what he'd said to Samantha.

"What is it, Son? Did I say something?"

"No! Your turn, Papa."

"All right. *Bueno.*" He made his move then.

Papa went to get a consoling cup of coffee, shoulders hunched over like he was eighty instead of forty, taking the cup over to the window, looking out, sighing, always that sigh.

"Oh, Papa! Don't make me feel guilty. What I want more than anything," Paolo said, "is to go out with the whales tomorrow."

"You know the doctor says no swimming for two weeks."

"But the whales'll be leaving. I need them."

"Why, Son?" Papa turned and looked into his eyes.

"Because I'm happy with them."

"And not with me?"

"You want to send me away." The words slipped out. He didn't want another fight, not now. "Sorry."

"Are you?"

Paolo shrugged. "Even Mama doesn't know why you're sending me to her. So why expect me to jump for joy?"

"She's just needling me. Leonora's really glad to have you. Anyhow, I wrote and said you'd read her letter. You'll be hearing from her."

"You told Mama I read your mail? Good, maybe she won't want a snoop around. Okay."

"She'll understand. Wait until you know her better."

The gentle tone in Papa's voice gave Paolo goose pimples. He did love her.

"I remember Mama very well. And we have something in common. We're content to stay strangers, but you—have this thing about getting me out of here—"

"After Luis almost killed you, I do, you're right, Son. Best thing in the world for you."

"Even if I'd hate it?"

"Even so, but you won't. Your mama likes a good time."

"Maybe you just want to send me so you can come visit, see her again yourself."

"So that's it! You think I'm using you? I can speak for myself if I want to, which, incidentally, I don't. Your move, Paolo." Papa came back and sat down, shaking his head, his face angry.

"Send me to school in Argentina. Please, Papa."

"I went away to school. I know what you'll gain."

"You're not me!"

"Are we playing checkers tonight or not?"

"So I should shut up, right? Okay, you've won, but

that doesn't mean what's good for you is good for me, Papa, and you have to think about that." Paolo stood up over the board and began picking up the checkers methodically, storing them in the wooden box with the sliding top. Poor sportsmanship. Awful. But wasn't it just one more thing, one more disaster, in this worst of all possible days? He felt tears in his eyes.

"Trust me. Please try to trust me in this."

Papa's voice was soft and tired, infinitely tired, as if raising one son, this particular son at least, had drained him terminally. Paolo was afraid to look up into his father's eyes, afraid of the disappointment he'd see.

"You could try trusting me for a change," Paolo snapped. He couldn't resist slamming the door to his room.

"I'm too sleepy," Paolo said the next morning when Papa woke him to go bird sketching. But when he heard the Jeep roar off, he got up, made himself *café con leche,* and sat at the front window dunking croissants in his coffee. Even they were no comfort. He'd never been so miserable!

At least it was Saturday and he didn't have to face Samantha or Luis. After Samantha told Luis, he probably wasn't speaking to him anyhow. Actually, he'd managed to fight with every single friend he had. He'd really done it this time! And it wasn't his fault, either!

Samantha lied when she said she loved him. Not lied exactly, but she sure didn't mean what he hoped.

Luis proved she was his territory. And Papa was trying to push him off on Mama. Who wouldn't prefer whales?

And in two weeks he'd be fourteen. Fourteen. All his life Papa had been saying that fourteen was virtually a man. "When you're fourteen, Son, you can swim with the whales. Wait until you're fourteen, Paolo, and then I'll teach you to drive. At fourteen you'll grow tall, wait and see." On and on like Hail Marys. And now it was beginning to look like fourteen might be the end of the world as he knew it.

Paolo finished his coffee and croissants, took the mug and plate back into the kitchen, and washed up before he braved the overcast sky and wind outside. He headed into the wind, walking fast, going toward a favorite flat rock down beyond the hotel that overlooked the bay. It was a place where the whales often came in close. He'd prefer to take the boat out and stay on board, but his head still bothered him some and it was too windy. He wasn't as foolhardy as Papa thought.

Paolo skirted the hotel and jogged on out to the point. There was a storm brewing. Good, let her blow. Storms were playtime for whales. He zipped his sweatshirt and pulled up the hood and sat on the rock, scanning the slate gray water. Choppy. A big school of fish off to the right. Plover and gulls dove for their dinners. Dolphins were jumping under the cliffs, silver arcs against white foam.

And the whales. Two blows close in, three more coming in. There was a whale using its tail as a sail, angled to the wind, and look at it come. He took a deep breath and exhaled salt air. Maybe Samantha and Papa thought he was a *malo*, but he could come here and watch a better life.

Then, right in front of him, a yearling whale suddenly breached, twenty tons leaping out of the water, paused an instant, and then, in a descending arc, crashed back into the bay, foam exploding like a geyser.

"A miracle," Paolo whispered.

And then another breached, and a third. "Showing off for the tourists, are you?"

And suddenly it was White Calf leaping into the air. He hovered a beautiful instant and crashed back into the sea.

"I knew you'd come! I knew it!" Paolo yelled. White Calf saw him sitting there. This was proof! And then he jumped up, calling, clapping and clapping, tears running down his face as White Calf breached and flipped and rolled. White Calf hadn't forgotten him.

"Wait for me! Wait for me!" Paolo called, nearly bursting his lungs as the calf and his mother submerged, disappearing into their own world, leaving him behind.

And then, suddenly, he had an idea. He yelled again but this time in the haunting voice of a whale. *"Mnnnnn, oooooooooom uuuuuooooom, mnnnnnnnnnmoh."*

Experts said whales could hear each other for miles. And the sound felt so wonderfully good coming up, up up from somewhere inside him. And he did sound like White Calf and his mother. He did! But even if they heard, would they understand he was asking them to wait until he could be with them again? *"Mnnnnnnnh. Uuuuuoooom. Oooooohhhm."*

He could only hope. And he could practice while he made spaghetti sauce for dinner. He'd sing along with their whale record. *"Mnnnnnnh. Uuuuuuooom. Ooooohhhm."* Tomorrow. Until tomorrow, my friend.

FIGHTING WITH SAMANTHA

10 Tuesday and Wednesday Luis didn't come to school, and Paolo didn't know if that made things better or worse. It was no easy matter not speaking to Samantha when you sat alone with her at a small table for six hours. Especially when Señora Martin thought Samantha was tutoring him. But okay. Samantha never wanted to speak to him again. Okay.

There was no school on Thursday so the Martins could celebrate an American holiday called Thanksgiving. This would have been a welcome respite except that the Martins invited Papa and him for dinner and a walk along the beach, the first Whale Camp visit since his concussion.

"Papa, my head aches like crazy. I'd better stay home," Paolo had said when he heard of the invitation.

"Here, take two aspirin. A day on the beach with elephant seals and the Martins will cure any headache."

And since he'd rather die than admit what he'd said to Samantha, he had to come. Especially the way things were between him and Papa. Papa had been polite as a stranger ever since black Monday, the day Paolo fought with everyone.

Thanksgiving morning was a scorcher. The two families struggled along the beach, the wind pelting them with hot sand, pushing Charley and Paolo to a jog. It was low tide, and the rocky flats between them and the surf were covered with mussels. Screeching gulls dove and picked up the mussels. They flew straight up and dropped them, smashing the shells, then they fought over the insides.

"Maybe we should hunt for a bomb shelter," Paolo said.

Charley grinned and put her hands over her ears. Spoonheart, the guanaco, loped along beside Paolo as they made their way north on the steep beach, trying to talk over the wind and the shrill cries of feasting gulls.

"He's doubled in size since I saw him!" Paolo shouted to Charley, acutely conscious of her older sister lagging behind, walking by herself.

"He drinks from a bucket."

"And eats everything in sight, and is especially fond of my petunias," added Señora Martin, overtaking them.

"But look at the way Spoonheart nuzzles Paolo, Mom. He never cuddles up to me, never. You should be a veterinarian too, animals love you so much."

Paolo shook his head. "I only want to watch, like

Papa. Maybe someday I'll write about how animals live. Spoonheart's showing you he won't be bossed around, that's all." He couldn't see or hear Samantha behind him but felt her presence with every step. Dr. Martin said she had to come, so she was straggling behind, in a foul mood and with a beastly headache, according to Charley. Strange. They'd both invented headaches and neither father believed them.

Then Spoonheart hung back, nibbling a patch of pampa grass, and Charley kept looking over her shoulder nervously.

"He'll come in his own sweet time," Paolo said. He didn't want to turn and look because he wouldn't give Samantha that satisfaction.

"Charlotte!" Señora Martin snapped as the guanaco turned back toward the house. Then she sprinted on ahead to catch up with the two fathers.

"He's fine. Don't worry so much," Paolo said.

"But I'm not sure the door is closed tight and he'll eat our dinner. Daddy says if I can't keep him in line, he'll have to go," Charley called back over her shoulder as she ran after the guanaco.

Paolo trudged along alone, walking tall, stomach in, in case Samantha was watching. Up ahead Señora and Dr. Martin and Papa were laughing together. About him and Samantha?

Down the beach he saw seals lying about companionably in groups. The penguins stood guard, one on each side of a depression in the ground where their newborn babies nested. Overhead a flock of plovers rode the currents. Out in the bay whales nursed their calves and dolphins frolicked.

Of all the creatures on this beach only he and Samantha chose to walk alone. Samantha chose to. He'd tried saying good morning, but she'd shrugged and stared through him. Knowing she was back there, deliberately avoiding him, hurt and angry, brought a rush of loneliness so overwhelming that he felt as if a good swift kick had knocked all the wind out of him.

Then, without a sound, she walked up beside him, still stone faced, still silent, but there.

Paolo couldn't help grinning. "Hi, Samantha."

She smiled too, a little half-smile but a whole lot better than nothing.

"I'm sorry, you know. And I've been thinking about what you said," Paolo began.

"Umm?"

"I was feeling like some kid you and Luis keep around for laughs—me and Charley."

Samantha nodded, pursing her lips. She still didn't say anything. Instead, she reached out and took his hand. Paolo started, pulling his hand a little, but Samantha hung on. His hand felt strange in her grasp, as if it had some pulse of its own, shooting tremors out to the rest of his body. He was afraid to look up. He didn't know if he wanted her to let go or not. They walked in silence for a while. Then she dropped his hand, and he felt terrible.

"The thing is, Luis *is* jealous of you and I do like you both." Samantha spoke in a friendly, matter-of-fact voice, as if they'd been talking all morning.

"Yeah, well—I like you a lot."

"I can't seem to help it. You notice things—oh, how the whales live, so many things Luis and I don't know and wish we did. But Luis and I have troubles you don't have, Gordo. He understands how I feel about losing my chance in swimming and I know how he feels about his mother. We have to stand up for ourselves, or maybe it's like Dad's always saying, to stand on our own two feet."

Paolo looked at Samantha. And you think I don't. Getting thrown out of your home didn't count? But why fight? Her smile made her face luminous, like sunlight. She'd said like, not love. Hadn't he known, really? "Friends?" he asked aloud.

Samantha nodded, grinning.

Paolo wished she'd take his hand again. He'd even have taken her hand if she hadn't brought up Luis. He knew she was watching him, but he couldn't look up, didn't know why. And she was standing so close. "I've missed you—a lot."

"Your fault."

He nodded, still not looking up. "Makes it worse."

"But I shouldn't have slapped you. First time I've ever done that. You really got to me, Gordo."

He looked up then and smiled. "Maybe I'm a cat-alyst for violence. Yesterday my only friend in the

world was White Calf. Hey, low tide. I'll race you to
the point and we can hunt crabs. Okay?"

Had he made her mad again? She looked so fierce,
and then suddenly her face cleared and she grinned.

"Okay, have it your way, Gordo. Let's go," and she
reached out her hand to him.

Paolo took it and had just time to feel once again
the strange warmth before she dropped his hand and
really started running for the point.

"Last one there is an idiot!" Samantha called back
over her shoulder.

For the rest of the day, as Samantha said, they played
at being the children their parents thought they were.
They hunted crabs, raced with Charley and Spoonheart, and rode horseback out to see newborn ostrich
chicks. And all the while Paolo had a sense of watching
himself, of time, of himself and Samantha playing to
delay something else.

Later that night, after what Señora Martin called a
semi-traditional Thanksgiving meal of chicken and
sweet potatoes, when they were eating the tasteless
pumpkin pie that seemed to mean so much to her
family, Paolo overheard Señora Martin talking softly
with Papa.

"Really, Raul, you should consider sending him on
with us for a while. Paolo would be company for Samantha, and I could help him catch up with any
schoolwork. He and his mother could get acquainted

gradually, to say nothing of perfecting his English."

"But Marian, that would mean two moves for the boy."

Paolo always hated it when Papa referred to him as the boy, which he did more and more lately.

"Two adventures!" Señora Martin knit steadily as she talked, working on a purple sweater for Charley. Samantha was embroidering another square for her quilt, this one of a penguin family. She would be ready to sew and tie the whole quilt in another few squares.

"But Leonora is expecting him. No, no, Marian, it's giving him choices that are bound to hurt both Paolo and Leonora—"

Paolo hardly breathed. They talked as if this *loco* business was all decided but the housing. How about what he wanted? Suppose he didn't recognize Mama at the airport? A school year! As long as a whale's migration. Longer.

Outside, the wind picked up and whooped around the little house, giving it the feeling of a refuge. And above the wind he heard the elephant seals, their gruff mournful calls familiar and lovable. This was his life, Papa was his family.

Dr. Martin spoke, clearing his throat. "Raul, I could use Paolo when we track gray whales to Baja this winter."

"Hey, please ask me, not Papa. Am I invisible or something? I'm not going! This is my home, Papa. You're my family."

Paolo felt them staring and found he was standing up, facing Papa. He'd knocked over his chair and stood there shouting. He set the chair back and sat down.

"Okay, relax. Nobody's going to kidnap you," Samantha said quietly.

"Paolo's right, he's right, everybody! It's not fair," Charley added, on her way to the front door with Spoonheart's latest mess. Spoonheart followed her out from the bathroom, curled up by Paolo's feet, and laid his head on his knees, as if he sympathized. Paolo patted him, watching his father, who kept darting glances at him, bewildered at his explosion. Well, nothing else seemed to penetrate.

"Looks like it's kids against adults," Señora Martin said with a laugh. "Think it over, Paolo. We'd love to have you."

"Son, it's only a migration. Whales do it every year. And I'll be your family wherever you are. Don't you realize that? Well, never mind. It's getting late, and ornithologists have to be up with the early birds. Time we were heading home." Papa put an arm around his shoulders and gave him a hug.

Then everyone started talking at once, too much and too heartily. Paolo's anger hung like a pall over the good-byes. He couldn't bring himself to thank either Dr. or Señora Martin for their offers. To Samantha he said, "They don't even listen to me."

"I know. But never mind that now. Ask your papa

if you can take me out swimming, okay? I want to swim with White Calf.''

"Indeed not, young lady," said Señora Martin.

"Oh, come now, Marian. The girl's earned the right to prove her swimming, and I took away her chance with the Junior Olympics. She's sensible and so's Paolo."

Samantha hugged her father. "Oh, Daddy, thank you, thank you forever," she said fervently.

Señora Martin sighed in a way that sounded just like Papa, Paolo thought.

"All right. I give up. Once."

"Hooray! I'll be careful, don't worry, Mom."

Papa hurried them outside. Paolo opened the car door and slumped against the seat with his eyes closed until they had been driving some minutes.

"Well, Son?"

"What I can't get over is that you don't listen, not to me and not to Mama. Why are you sending him, she says?"

"But she wants you, always has. Tried to take you when she left, but I couldn't stand losing you both and she gave in. She felt sorry for me, I suppose. Would you rather stay with the Martins, until you get to know Leonora?"

"No. That's not the point."

His father sighed monumentally and nodded.

"Why didn't Mom ask me to visit before this?"

"When she left, I asked her not to interfere for a while. Look, Son, I find this damn painful—"

"Papa, you've asked me to leave home. Tell me."

"Oh, God, not leave home. Just go off to school like I did. And to your mother, at that. All right! I was in love with your mother and she walked out on me. So I wanted time to get over it. Okay? And as for her letters, there's one for you in the mail I picked up this morning."

"My own letter! And you didn't give it to me?"

"I thought you'd have a better day—if I waited—until we got home."

"Next time let me decide, please."

Nothing further was said during the half-hour drive home to Puerto Piramides. His letter, and Papa wasn't even sorry! A wall had slammed down between them. Papa would call this another stalemate. Maybe Mama couldn't take so many stalemates and that's why she left?

At home they said good night formally. Paolo was in bed when Papa came into his room.

"Here's your letter, Son," he said, and handed over an air-mail letter that smelled faintly of lavender. Paolo tore it open.

Queriod Paolo, My Dearest Son,
    I have been waiting to write until I had some idea whether *you* might wish to visit me or the

idea was just a whim of your papa's. To see you would be such a joy. I would so hate to find that you weren't happy to see me, and so disappointed. After all, why should you want to visit a stranger, even if she is your mother? Still, I dream of you. I see us meeting, a bit awkward with each other here in San Francisco, walking together in the park, getting acquainted over a hot fudge sundae. I want so much to know you and have you meet San Francisco and your American mother. It's been too long and I regret that—terribly. Please come. But Paolo, do get Papa to tell you a little about our separation so that won't be left to me. He'd rather die, but it would do him good. And then you and I can start fresh and free.

Your loving Mama

THE RESCUE

11 But what had Mama wanted Papa to tell him? And how was he supposed to answer her letter? Paolo wondered two days later as he walked across the beach under a dawn sky, following Luis and Samantha.

"Son, it's so long ago. Why dredge up the pain again? Leonora was a city girl who was desperately lonely here. She wanted me to move to San Francisco, but this is where I have to live and work," Papa had said when he asked.

"That's *all*?"

"That's the gist of it. Ask your mama if you're so curious," Papa had snapped, slamming his bedroom door.

Forget it, Paolo told himself as he hurried to catch up with Samantha and Luis. Samantha and he wore their wet suits, but Luis had his slung over his shoulder. The doctor finally said Paolo could swim again, and miraculously Papa agreed to let him go out with Luis and Samantha.

They walked separately. The relationship between

the three of them was shifting, and no one of them knew quite where they stood. Paolo knew Luis suspected Samantha of favoring him since the fight. If only it were true! Samantha hated making either Luis or himself unhappy, that was all. He watched her walking on ahead, scuffing the sand, digging her toes into its warmth.

"I have a right to swim with the whales too, so why does this silence make me feel guilty?" she asked as Paolo caught up to her.

"Hey, you're going to have a great time. We all are. Relax." Paolo turned and waited for Luis.

Without a word, Luis and Paolo untied the skiff and then, one on each side, they pushed the boat across the beach and into the surf. Samantha jumped in and they followed. Paolo started the motor, set it on slow, and headed out toward the middle of the bay.

There was only a light breeze, and the steady putt-putt of the motor was soothing. Paolo rested, watching the terns and gulls diving for fish. Forget all the rest. Luis and Samantha were his friends, and they were going out to the whales on a perfect day.

The salmon sky reflected like iridescence on the water. Paolo saw Samantha's face ease as she breathed deeply of the salt air. Luis's shoulders lost that stiff look and his face relaxed. Paolo smiled, and Luis and Samantha smiled back easily.

"Wind's dropped," Luis said.

"Oooh, I could live out here," Samantha cried, throwing her arms wide.

"Says a girl who hates eating fish," said Paolo, who often wished the same thing.

"Mermaids are probably vegetarian."

"More likely a species of shark."

"Thank you, Gordo! Where's the famous White Calf?"

Paolo only shrugged, but he scanned the horizon anxiously. Whales had started leaving the bay, migrating to northern feeding grounds, and White Calf and his mother could have gone. The big males had cleared out, and every day there were fewer mothers and calves left. It had been a week since he'd seen them. They could have gone.

"White Calf and his mother have come to the boat before—that's all I can say. It's late in the season."

"Seeing's believing," said Luis.

"Oh, great, now I'm a liar if they don't show."

"No, but you should have brought me out earlier, that's all," Samantha said.

"*Sí*, over the dead body of your mother."

They fell silent again, each scanning the horizon, finding blows and the arcs of playful dolphins but no whales surfacing. About twenty minutes out, Paolo thought he caught a glimpse of a white hump breaking the water's surface, then a larger dark back emerged, in the distance but heading toward them. He cut the engine and waited.

"Is—?"

"Don't know. But you'll see whales, Samantha."
He grinned and pointed.

"I thought you'd run out of gas," said Luis, easing
into his wet suit. Then he reached out and grabbed
Samantha's hand. "Glad you came, *querida?*"

"Oh, how much I've wanted to come! Thank you
both."

Paolo tried to keep his eyes on the whales, all too
aware of Luis and Samantha's clasped hands.

"Is it your pet whale, Gordo?"

"Could be White Calf, but he's nobody's pet. I'd like
you to meet him, Luis."

"How do you know it's a him?"

"I don't. *Difícil*, hard to tell. I have to say something,
don't I?"

"Stick up for men," said Samantha.

They all smiled. It was too peaceful a morning to
bicker, the bay turning a deep turquoise under the
rising sun. And through the flurry of birds and fish,
they could see two whales moving slowly but steadily
toward them.

Soon Paolo was sure. He could see the white back
and the larger gray-brown back clearly now. Then
suddenly, the white whale leapt half out of the water,
breaching, greeting them in a storm of spray and
then, with an explosion of water, White Calf sank back
into the bay.

"He really knows you," Luis whispered, awed.

"That's him. What a show-off!" Paolo replied proudly.

And soon the two whales were with them, so close they could hear the soft *whoosh, whoosh* of their breathing when they surfaced. The mother kept a little distance, watching her calf, staying between him and the boat. White Calf seemed as glad to see them as Paolo was to see him, turning their way whenever he leapt out of the water, breaching again and again with flamboyant abandon, splashing thunderously.

"Hey, he sprayed me. I'm all wet." Samantha laughed.

"I thought you said he came up to the boat, swam under us, and let you touch him," Luis said.

Paolo frowned at Samantha for telling Luis he touched the whales and was pleased to see that she dropped Luis's hand. Did she tell him *everything*? "His mother knows there are strangers."

"Strangers? Gordo, I'm out here one hell of a lot more than you are. I'm no stranger!" Luis tugged at his wet suit and, before Paolo could stop him, went over the side.

"*Estúpido!* Come back, Luis."

"Will he spook the whales?" asked Samantha.

"Could. But we can't leave him alone. Ready?" Paolo let down the anchor.

"Anytime," Samantha said.

Paolo checked the anchor to make sure it was holding

and nodded to Samantha to go ahead. She slid smoothly over the side. Her long blond hair fanned out in the water. Fortunately she was a first-rate swimmer. He wouldn't have to worry about her.

"Oh, damn," he muttered, swimming fast. Luis knew better than to swim toward whales, especially calling out like that, showing off for Samantha. He'd spook that mother. Sometimes he just went crazy.

Luis looked around and called to Samantha, but she shook her head. Good. Paolo beckoned angrily at Luis, trying to get him to turn around without shouting and further startling the mother. When he saw this wouldn't work, he swam faster. "I'll bring him back," he said quietly, passing Samantha.

She nodded and turned on her back, floating, saving her energy.

Paolo plowed through the water desperately, trying to reach Luis before he did something crazy. The mother was watching, alert. Then she cried out, one long haunting moan, and Luis did stop.

Thank God, Paolo thought.

But then White Calf began moving ever so slowly, toward Luis. Paolo felt a quick pang of jealousy. The calf wanted to know Luis. He was curious. Well, since White Calf had grown used to himself, why shouldn't he trust other humans? Luis, as if mesmerized, turned again and began to swim very slowly toward the calf. They seemed drawn to each other, Luis and White Calf. As if they were magnetized.

Suddenly the mother whale flipped her tail, only a flick, but the two-ton tail hit the water with an explosion, which left a churning mass of foam. And as the foam settled Paolo couldn't find Luis. Anywhere! He'd disappeared into the inky depths, caught in the riptide of that tail. Damn, he'd drown!

Paolo swam like he'd never swum before, stroking long and deep. When he reached the spot where he'd last seen Luis, he dove. As he fought his way down he caught glimpses of Luis below him, struggling to rise.

Just as he felt excruciating pressure in his own lungs he reached him, but in that moment, Luis went limp and started to fall. Paolo grabbed the back of his wet suit first, got one arm around his chest and neck from behind, and stroked for the surface with the other arm, his lungs bursting.

Up, up, up! Would he make it? Could he reach the surface before his own lungs gave out? Exploded. Before his arms dropped off. Just a little more—it was getting light, lighter—a school of little silver fish all around them—and then he broke surface, sunlight, ears popping, a deep draft of fresh air. He was out, breathing, sunlight, breathing. He was alive!

He still had Luis in an anchor grip around the chest, and he checked to see he wasn't choking him. God, he was heavy. Could he get him back to the boat?

He gulped air, paddling with his feet and one arm

until he could breathe easily again. "Luis, Luis, can you hear me, help me, help me," he whispered hoarsely.

Samantha swam up and took Luis's wrist. "He's got a pulse, I think. What do you want me to do?"

"Just stay with us." He hoped Samantha was right about Luis having a pulse, but he couldn't do anything about that now, not until he got him into the boat, couldn't even worry about how he'd get him in, just get him there, just keep his head above water.

He could see the skiff, like a white beacon under the sun, and he headed for it. He could hear Samantha talking but only registered the soothing tone of her voice as she swam alongside. He could feel each stroke bringing them closer to the boat even as the arm around Luis felt ready to drop off. Luis's wet suit chaffed his arm painfully. If only he could change arms. If only Luis could come to and help. Was he still alive? If only Samantha could take a turn. He couldn't take the chance, was afraid to risk handing him over. What about the whales? Well, what about them?

"What now?" Sanantha asked.

He looked up and saw that they were at the boat. He nearly dropped Luis in his surprise, relief, exhaustion. God, it was a long way to lift him. But he'd be damned if he'd lose him, not after this, not now.

"Samantha, can you hold him while I get in the

boat?'' It would be simpler than explaining balancing the boat and having her try to pull.

"Yes. I passed lifesaving."

"Sure?"

She only noded, moving in to take Luis from behind, and when Paolo felt she had him firmly, he gradually, reluctantly let go. Then the relief was enormous. He felt like he could fly.

Once in the boat, he dared to look down. Samantha still had Luis and seemed to be trying to burp water out of him. "Good for you. Now, I'm going to brace myself and try to haul him in." Oh, God, don't let me capsize, he prayed.

At that moment Luis started to cough. He was alive, regaining consciousness! Thank God. Samantha kept talking, soothing, telling him to help, he'd nearly drowned, Luis coughing, vomiting water, reaching one arm up to Paolo as Samantha told him, Paolo grabbing hold, water pouring out of Luis.

"Give me your other arm, Luis. The other one, too, the right arm. Please," Paolo called to his friend. And when he had both hands tight, "Samantha, quick, get in the other side—for ballast."

And Samantha was way ahead of him, already balancing the boat, hanging on the other side, hoisting herself over the side and in. "Now," she said.

"Can you help me, Luis?"

"Momentito."

All right, he could wait a moment. Thank God the water was calm. Luis finished coughing and hoisted himself, feebly, but it was enough so Paolo could grab one leg as he let go of an arm and heave him on board.

"We made it," Paolo said, easing Luis into the bottom of the boat, propping sweatshirts against his back to keep him on his side before falling back onto a seat himself. That's it, he thought. It's all over. He found he was shaking.

"Gordo saved your life," Samantha said to Luis.

"Gracias," said Luis weakly, and then vomited more water.

He lay in the bottom of the boat, a tall dark boy with the finely chiseled features of a Spanish explorer, white faced and still as a corpse, except for his chest, which was rising and falling, rising and falling— breathing as hard as a fish that's just been landed, Paolo thought.

"You did, you know. You saved his life and could have lost your own, Gordo. You know that?" Samantha asked.

Paolo heard her, but he wondered why she was saying this now, now when Luis already felt awful. What did it matter, anyhow? "We all made it," he said. "I couldn't have done it without you."

Samantha grinned. "I know you couldn't and it makes me feel good, like a champion. Did you notice, the whales are gone?"

Paolo scanned the water and nodded sadly. Would White Calf and his mother ever trust him again? And would he be able to accept the whales with such carefree confidence? Or was this the real loss? That rare and trusting friendship with creatures from another world. He sighed and, infinitely weary, reached out and pulled up the anchor.

"We'd better get you back to the doctor, *amigo*," he said, starting the motor.

IT'S A FREE OCEAN, ISN'T IT?

12 "I'm going home. I'll take a nap and that's all," Luis said as they struggled back across the beach toward town.

"Luis, you fainted. You could have a concussion," Samantha insisted.

Luis shrugged.

He looked exhausted, drained, a little green in the face to Paolo. He might be all right if he went home and rested for the afternoon. Still, who could forget the baker who'd nearly drowned off Whale Camp, laughed it off, then came down with pneumonia and died?

"We better see the doctor. You have to stay well— for your mama, Luis," Paolo finally said quietly. He felt himself flush, for he knew Luis would do what he said today and he didn't want to abuse this new trust. "Samantha has to tell her family, anyhow."

It was Samantha's turn to flush. "Charley'll tell."

Still Luis shook his head. "Doctors cost money. Mama needs one more than I do."

Papa could pay, Paolo thought, but with Luis's pride that would only make things worse.

"Dr. Oliva won't charge *you*," Samantha said.

"Meaning he'll treat me like the charity case you think I am, *querida?*"

They'd reached the road and turned right toward the clinic. Paolo hoped Samantha would shut up because Luis had turned along with them. Best way to get Luis to do something was to let the subject drop.

Samantha must have noticed because she silently hooked her arm through Luis's arm and, when they came to the clinic, turned in.

They found Dr. Oliva and Paolo's father playing chess on the examining table. Dr. Martin was there too, kibitzing.

"Back already, Paolo?" Papa asked, moving his knight.

"How do right whales stack up against the grays, Samantha?" asked Dr. Martin. "You look done in, kids."

"Whole *loco* town's here," Luis muttered.

"Wind came up," Paolo said.

"Oh, whales are all great," Samantha said quietly.

Dr. Oliva kept glancing at Luis, who was looking pretty green. "To what do we owe the honor of your visit, *jóvenes?*"

"Just a little accident. A sudden current sucked me under. Gordo saved me. I'm fine, but they insisted I come." Luis shrugged.

Paolo thought the adults' faces all wore the same expression—concern and skepticism in about equal parts.

"A sudden current?" Dr. Martin nervously brushed his hand over his stray hairs.

"How do you feel, Luis?" Dr. Oliva asked, shushing the other questions.

"He passed out," Samantha said.

Paolo's father raised his eyebrows. "Really sucked you under—quite a current, then. Strange for November, no?"

Dr. Oliva picked up the chessboard and carefully set it on a filing cabinet. "Please. Why don't the lot of you go on in the kitchen and ask Maria Louisa for some *café con leche* while I take the smallest look at this young man?" He opened the door to the kitchen, where his wife sat at a big round table correcting third-grade papers, and made shooing noises until everyone left his office. "*Gracias*, Maria," he said, shutting the door behind them.

"Luis roared like a lion when Dr. Oliva wanted to keep him overnight, didn't he?" Paolo asked later as he was helping his father chop onions for *polenta*. It was the *viejo*'s turn to cook, but Paolo wanted to learn to cook *polenta* so they could have it more often. Papa was getting lazy about good dinners lately.

"Well, Luis should have stayed overnight at the clinic—no one to watch him at home. But I understand he's worried about his mama. He'd better make sure he gets checked again tomorrow, that's all. By the way, what did happen out there today, Son?"

Paolo wasn't fooled by Papa's casual tone. He looked up into the older man's stern eyes.

"Luis said you saved his life. Quite an admission for him! Why, when that boy swims like a fish?"

Paolo nodded, then shrugged. Papa would hear from the Martins, anyhow. "He drifted a bit too close to a nervous whale and she flipped her tail a little, that's all."

"That's all?"

Paolo couldn't tell if there was irony in his father's tone or not but decided to treat it like a straight question. "That's all. *Nada*, really."

"Nothing? I've seen boats the size of this room smashed by the flip of a whale's tail. You could've been killed, Son."

Paolo shook his head. He set to work on the green peppers, giving the chopping his full attention.

"And Samantha said he was unconscious—must have weighed a ton. And I'll bet he was chasing the whale, showing off for her. Don't tell me no, Paolo! A boy who blushes and can't meet my eyes when he lies had better stick to the truth. Luis needs—well, a father for starters, but I don't want you risking your neck over his frustrations again. Understand?"

Paolo nodded. "Luis needs a job that pays better and lets him stay in school."

"Then why wasn't he looking for one today? Lucky for that macho kid you keep your wits about you and swim like a powerhouse. I don't suppose he thanked you?" Papa put one arm affectionately around his shoulders and pulled him close.

"He did. I couldn't have gotten him into the boat without Samantha, though." He felt the color rising in his face and bent over the tomatoes, chopping them very fine.

"Luis wouldn't have had anyone to show off for without her either, would he?"

Paolo decided to drop the subject and silently watched his father stir the vegetables with the browned meat. Then he crumbled some herbs and tossed them in.

"Secret's in simmering the sauce before adding the cornmeal. Takes time."

"I've got time."

To Paolo, his father seemed unusually preoccupied all that evening. He burned the *polenta*, lost his glasses three times, let his pipe go out, and then couldn't find his lighter. Worst of all, he kept hopping back up the minute he sat down and wandering over to stare out the window. Paolo beat him easily at checkers in spite of being so tired he could hardly stay awake. In spite of aching in every muscle. Was the *viejo that* worried he might have drowned trying to pull Luis in? Or that annoyed with Luis? He thought it better not to ask

and had already gone to bed when his father came
into his room and dropped yet another letter on the
bed.

"So this is why you were so jumpy?"

"This came from your mother today. Thought it
might explain better than I could. And she makes an
odd suggestion—for Leonora. Well, sleep well, Son."

"Fat chance, with this. I still haven't answered her
letter to me."

"I know what you mean. Well, good night, Paolo."

And Papa closed the door behind him before Paolo
recovered enough to ask why he kept dropping these
bombshells. Hadn't today been long enough? He knew
the answer, anyhow.

Papa wanted him to read these letters, but he'd
rather die than talk about them. That was why he'd
left the first note open on the kitchen table. Paolo
sighed, reaching for the lavender-scented envelope,
addressed to Papa.

"What now, Leonora?" he asked aloud.

13 By the following morning Paolo had memorized his mother's latest and longest letter
and knew he had to get out of the house. He had no
idea where he was going, but he couldn't speak to
Papa. Not yet. Not until he knew where he was.

It was Papa's habit to be out walking by dawn so
he could sketch the waking birds. So Paolo had to
leave with the first gray light. He rolled two changes
of clothing, a sweater, matches, a flashlight, and a first-
aid kit into his sleeping bag. He couldn't risk sneaking
into the kitchen for provisions, so he took his birthday
money to buy food.

When he started down the hill, he'd made no decision except getting out so he wouldn't have to face
Papa. Hunger made him head in the direction of Luis's
adobe *casita*. Luis's mother slept late these days, so
he'd be alone. He could grab a bite to eat and then
leave the sleeping bag while he went back for his horse.
After Papa had gone.

When they were younger, Paolo threw gravel at the

window to wake his friend, and he did so this morning. Luis opened the window.

"God, Gordo, it's not even light."

"I know, but I'm hungry."

Then he heard the bolt on the door squeak open. As long as he could remember, Luis's house had been locked up and theirs had been left open, though they had things worth stealing and Luis and his mother had nothing. The older boy looked at the sleeping bag but said only, "What do you want—eggs or leftover *polenta?*"

"Both, *gracias.*"

Luis built a fire in the old woodstove, and in a few minutes the room was warm and fragrant with the aroma of bubbling *polenta* and frying eggs. Luis was getting to be a good cook. Paolo closed his eyes and leaned on the sleeping bag. He didn't want to think yet. Not about Papa, not about the letter, not about Mama or her proposal.

"Want to go for a swim?" Luis asked as he dished out generous portions.

Paolo considered. Luis looked pale but basically all right this morning. Still, he must have swallowed a lot of water yesterday. "Why so soon?"

"I want White Calf and his mama to understand I'm a friend before they leave our bay. I'll stay in the boat if you want. Just so I see White Calf. Please, Gordo?"

Paolo nodded and started eating. He didn't feel like talking, but the turmoil inside him eased a little when he thought of going out on the bay. Gliding through clear water—floating free and easy—and maybe they'd see White Calf. Maybe nothing had changed.

"All right?" Luis asked.

But Paolo shook his head slowly. Too dangerous. He had too much on his mind. "Too risky with the mother whale. And I ache in every bone in my body. Another day, all right?"

Luis nodded sadly. "Maybe his mama still doesn't like me today? Maybe next week she'll forgive me?"

"Maybe. You must ache too." They ate in silence. Paolo understood Luis. He needed to feel White Calf come to him again. He needed the mother to accept him as she had Paolo. But not yet.

Luis kept watching him, but as he finished eating asked only, "You okay?"

Paolo shrugged. Through the open window he heard their Jeep sputter and start. Papa was off to sketch penguins. Regular as clockwork. "Now I'm okay. Good eggs."

"What you needed today, huh?"

"Saved my life," Paolo said, surprised at Luis's understanding.

"That bad?"

There was irony in Luis's voice. Paolo looked up suspiciously, his stomach tightening. That's the way it always began. They'd get to talking and something would set him off. Well, not today. He looked Luis straight in the eyes. "What is it with you?"

There was a long silence. They stared at each other, neither giving way. Finally Luis shrugged.

"Mama. She's worse. I can't do a thing. Gordo, trouble's written all over your face. It's tough. But at least your papa's healthy and earns money. You saved my life yesterday and now you say I've saved yours by heating up *polenta*. Some bad joke or maybe you're reminding me?"

"I didn't mean it that way. You'd have saved me. Your mama's great." Luis was always older and stronger, and being saved was humiliating. And Paolo did feel bigger—like he could do so much more—after yesterday. That was true.

Luis's face had softened. "Great is right," he said, nodding, pushing his black hair back out of his face.

"Luis, your mama needs you and she loves you. My mama left when I was a year old."

"So? My papa never even showed his dumb face."

"So, how would you like it if you suddenly had to go live with him?"

Luis said nothing for a few minutes, staring out the window, and then he turned back. "It would depend on what he's like. He and Mama didn't get along, but I always thought he and I might make out fine together."

"But wouldn't you feel—weird—seeing him? Kind of like you'd been kicked in the stomach by a horse?"

Luis shrugged. "I might. But I'd like to find out. He's part of me that I haven't met, and we could—he's my papa, Gordo! You and your papa have a fight?"

"He calls it a stalemate." Paolo grinned. "It's Mama who's got me spinning like a top. Hey, I'm going back for my horse. Want me to put the sleeping bag outside so you can go on to school?"

"I'll wait for you, but hurry it up. I promised Samantha I wouldn't be late anymore."

"I'm not going today."

"Gordo, super-student, cutting. Running away?"

Paolo shook his head. For a minute they looked at each other, taking stock.

"Take it easy, *amigo*." Luis's voice was gentle and brought tears to Paolo's eyes.

"Thanks. You too." He walked up the path to his house without looking back, hurrying to get Pancho while Papa was out sketching. When he returned with the horse, a salami and bread packed in the saddlebags, he found his sleeping bag on the porch. Luis had packed him a lunch, two sandwiches and an orange, neatly wrapped in a clean white dish towel.

Paolo stared at the sandwiches. Then he turned and looked for Luis, already far down the road, almost to the school. To Samantha. Leaving him here alone, more alone than he'd ever been before, ever in his life. Maybe he should go on to school and sit around with Samantha and Luis. Talk it over with them. Luis used to say he hated his papa, but now he'd be willing to meet him. He could leave after school.

The horse nickered, restless.

"You're right, Pancho. Make a clean break. Leave her to Luis."

Still Paolo hesitated. He looked up into the red dawn, a line of pelicans stretching from one horizon to the other, nothing on their minds but a school of fish. Maybe he'd come back as a pelican if he had another life. He'd make a pretty good pelican, except he'd hate migrating.

"Well, Pancho, we've got to stick together, *amigo*, understand," he said as he swung up onto the stocky criollo horse. "Giddap!"

He rode slowly out of courtesy to the old horse. There was no hurry. Papa wouldn't be back for an hour. No wind. Good to ride without bracing against a stinging blast of sand. Riding away from that spidery handwriting, the letter he'd left on the kitchen table, the new picture it gave of his mother. And of Papa, Raul to her, a stranger to Paolo.

Mama had written,

> It appears that we've made rather a muddle of it, Raul. Not in ways either of us totally understand, perhaps, but enough to make me wonder if we shouldn't at least see each other again. Make some decision. Either divorce or give up

the idea. I do feel fortunate to have a chance to know Paolo before I'm a mother of the groom, and I thank you for what I'm, grudgingly, coming to see is your sacrifice.

You said, so long ago, that you didn't want to be friends if we couldn't be a family. You felt it better for Paolo and necessary for us to make a clean break, as I recall, so we could put the marriage behind us and get on with life. Particularly since we still cared for each other but neither of us could live where—and to some extent how—the other wanted.

I've only come once in a dozen years, though I've wanted to come, heaven knows. I've yearned to see our son as he grows up. It has been a loss I will never get over. And Paolo has suffered, I'm sure. And now you and Paolo may repeat our anguish unless we think this move through from his point of view.

Not, my still beloved, that I regret for a moment leaving that skull-strewn desert of yours, but perhaps civilization has penetrated even Patagonia by now and these last dozen years have certainly made me more tolerant. And it's Paolo's world. His whole and beloved world.

So why don't you come up with our son for a visit, to help settle Paolo and me? After all, he must think I deserted him. And that you're deserting, and possibly booting him out, now.

There was more. Descriptions of half a dozen jobs Mama had held. None had worked out until her graphics started selling and she could wash her hands of offices. *Oh, the relief,* she wrote.

Papa thought *this* letter would answer questions? What did Mama want? Family or a divorce? To come home to the peninsula or live in San Francisco? And Papa? What kind of man would say she couldn't visit their son unless they were a family?

Anyhow, one thing he had to admit. She'd wanted him, all these years, and now, too. Only she was seeing how it was for him, how he was feeling. She wasn't even here and she understood perfectly! Papa was here all the time and blindly demanded Paolo go away to school like he had. To become him.

Papa never asked what *he* wanted, that was for sure! Still, Papa had sounded so loving when he said, "Leonora would have liked Señora Martin." And why did Papa give him the letter to read when it made him look bad? Why, why, why did they both want him to go halfway around the world when he and Papa were doing fine the way they were? And Mama too!

The horse slowed and stopped to nibble at an outcropping of beach grass. Paolo waited a few minutes and then nudged him in the ribs. "Hey, Pancho, get a move on. We haven't got *all day*, you know!"

ON HIS OWN

14 Paolo headed for his favorite beach, one he'd found by accident when he fell down a hillside years ago. The beach itself was steep and rocky, bordering a shallow inlet on the north coast, home to penguins and sea lions. No outsider seemed to go there except for occasional killer whales in search of dinner. No one would think to look for him there, and he'd be safe. Good thing he'd left a note so Papa wouldn't worry. He hadn't said where he was or how long he'd be gone. He didn't know.

The breeze was balmy, carrying the tang of salt and geraniums. The sun felt warm on his back and the surf was its own music. Maybe he could lie out under the sun and the stars for a few days, play with the penguins, and forget—or find a way to live with this new father, and a resurrected mother. He liked that word, resurrected.

He'd always heard that what Mama loved was the music of good conversation in San Francisco, but these letters showed she'd be pretty broken up if he didn't come. She had missed him and *wanted* to see him.

144

Strange about Papa wanting no contact—he'd never *seemed* bitter.

Better think of something else—the purple carpet of ice plant sprouting again since the rain, penguin nests, White Calf drifting in his mother's shadow, sunlight seeping through the water. White Calf depended on *his* mother! He didn't know his father, though. Like Luis.

When it came right down to it, maybe there wasn't much use in thinking about *anything*; better to ride along, letting the sun and the good smell of a salty sea sink into his bones, letting Pancho pick out their way.

But wasn't it curious how you could drift along happily for years and then whammo—it was all gone! Mama had been a daydream, a photo on the wall. Papa was always there, making dinner, playing checkers, sketching birds. Two guys who got along but never realized they didn't know each other. So, now what? And what could he write to Mama?

As Paolo came to the steep path leading down to the beach, he dismounted and let Pancho graze the sprouting grasses before starting down. No fodder on the beach. He'd have to remember to bring the old horse up to graze the hillside again tonight.

He counted four harems of sea lions and half a dozen clumps of elephant seal pups on the rocky beach. And the beach was black and white with penguins waddling down to the water for fish, taking turns sitting on their nests, braying conversationally. At least a thousand penguins. Eggs must be hatching because penguins stood guard against robber gulls beside each nest carved into the roots of bushes. A flock of pink flamingos waded along the shore of the inlet, stilt legged, stalking sand crabs.

This was the world he understood. Thank God he'd come! He felt a great black cloud of gloom lifting, and he wanted to get on down. Whistling for Pancho, he started down the steep path, urging the reluctant horse with frequent tugs on the reins.

Once on the beach, Paolo braved the rising wind and gathered wood for a fire. He chose a campsite behind a large outcropping of rock for protection during the night. It was chilly this afternoon and sure to get windier after dark.

When he had enough wood, he rolled out the sleeping bag and, lying down, fell almost immediately into an uneasy sleep.

It was late afternoon when he wakened. Sleepily he walked down to the water to wash. He really should gather more wood, just to be on the safe side. As he approached the stilt-legged flamingos rooting in the surf, they suddenly flew up in a body, with a great loud fluttering of pink wings. They circled overhead, squawking as if pursued by devils. Had he caused all that?

Then he caught his breath. Cruising the inlet, not fifty feet away, was a sleek black-and-white killer whale, its big back fin slicing slowly through the water. The fin was taller than Paolo. What a treat!

He searched the inlet carefully for more fins, since killer whales weren't solitary creatures, usually traveling in pods of a half dozen or so—but this one appeared to be quite alone. The lagoon was shallow. Another killer whale would have to surface to breathe every few minutes and there wasn't a ripple. Awesome in its silky black-and-white simplicity, there was no creature more beautiful. Each sighting seemed a miracle. And he'd never seen their teeth. Maybe today.

The flamingos, safely airborne, circled the inlet sounding the alarm, again and again, and finally flew off down the coast. Let them go. He'd much rather see a killer whale. He pulled a poncho over his head and, chewing on a hunk of bread, settled down to watch.

He'd never seen a killer whale so close. The king of the ocean with skin smooth as silk. Not a scar or an incrustation on him. Of course, like dolphins, they didn't collect the barnacles and parasites that most whales did.

The black fin drifted slowly toward a patch of beach where a harem of sea lions lay sunning themselves at the edge of the surf. Several of the young sea lions who had been swimming a little way out had come rushing back to shore when the dominant male bellowed the alarm. They scrambled onto the rocks while the harem moved farther back up the steep beach, squealing and tumbling over one another, comical in their hurry. They weren't taking any chances. Only the killer whale glided serenely and silently through the inlet.

Two straggling sea lion pups struggled out of the water, hurrying after the rest of the harem.

Suddenly, though he saw nothing, Paolo heard a thin despairing cry, eerie in the silence. The fearful cry vibrated in the air and hung over the beach, silencing birds and animals alike. And then he saw a sea lion pup thrown high in the air, and then falling into a jagged cone of teeth, the monstrous mouth clamping shut in an instant. So quickly, so totally over, that Paolo couldn't be sure he'd actually seen it happen. But he could hear the whimpering of that other sea lion pup who had made it to the slippery beach, sliding and inching forward, gradually working his way toward the safety of the harem.

And then he saw that the killer whale himself had come half up onto the beach—in lurching after the sea lion pup the huge mammal had stranded himself! He must be thirty feet long. Paolo could see clearly that steel gray eye, saw it blink, saw the trembling rippling over that black-and-white hide.

"Oh, no," Paolo cried, terrified for him, sure the great whale was doomed.

Then, ever so slowly, the whale wiggled its surprisingly supple hulk back through the sand, back through the surf, and on into the deeper water, like an old bull elephant seal.

And then, with a lazy arc, the sleek giant turned over onto his back, ridding himself of sand, taking his ease after a meal. He'd made it back to sea in so few minutes that the whole episode seemed like a dream.

But it was real enough to the other sea lion pup, still clambering up onto higher land with the harem, still squealing with fright. The killer whale surfaced, rolled over again, and then sank until only the tall black fin sailed above the surface. He slowly drifted down the inlet toward the open sea, serene and silent—his hunger satisfied.

The beach was as it had been, penguins braying and the sea lions sleeping, and it was hard to believe he'd seen the whale strike. Only the memory of that despairing cry remained real. That and the black fin like a sail far down the inlet. Papa said they sometimes found as many as half a dozen seal pups in a killer whale's belly. He wiped away tears. His hands and legs were shaking. He felt sick to his stomach. What was wrong with him?

He knew killer whales didn't attack people, were in fact friendly. He wasn't afraid, just shaken. Anyway, they had to eat and he ate steaks, didn't he? He remembered feeding mice to a fox family. He remembered watching their cat drag a headless sparrow into the house and lay it proudly before his father, the ornithologist, who only told the cat that mice tasted better.

He watched some penguins waddle back down to the wet sand, listing from side to side. They slid into the surf, so confident in the water that they ignored the black killer whale still sunning himself farther out in the inlet. Then, as he watched, the killer whale drifted toward the opening of the shallow inlet, and in a few minutes he'd gone back to the open sea, back to his own kind. Paolo sat on the beach until the sun slid down over the horizon. He knew it would be dark soon and his flashlight wouldn't last long. His only real light would come from a fire, and he'd better get it started.

Or go home. Somehow, since the killer whale strike, he felt lonely.

His hand shook as he held a match to the dry grass. But when the flame shot up and caught quickly on the driftwood he began to feel better, to lose the sadness that hung over him. The fire looked cheerful. The evening star was out. And he had the stick of salami and a loaf of bread that he'd taken when he'd gone back for his horse. For once he'd have as much salami sandwich as he wanted. And he'd brought a jug of water and some cocoa. What a feast!

Plenty to share. Why didn't he think to ask someone—Luis or Samantha—to come along? Samantha's mother wouldn't let her come, that's why. His father was most likely over at the Martins' this very minute and they were all sympathizing with him. Awful Gordo, worrying Papa.

And Luis was taking care of his mama. It would have been good to talk more about his father, about wanting to know him. Because there was a part of Paolo that wanted to know Mama, particularly lately. Not that he was all that eager to live with her in California, but like Luis said, she was part of him. He liked the way she imagined them having a hot fudge sundae together, a little awkward with each other at first.

Then there was Samantha. Samantha with the golden hair and those direct blue eyes. She'd know how he was feeling—and hearing his own voice tell her about the letter, he'd understand better. And then maybe she'd take his hand again and . . .

Paolo stared into the fire as the sky darkened into the long Patagonian twilight. Time seemed to stand still.

Penguins waddled down to the water, caught fish, and came back to relieve mates on the nest, giving a pattern to the dusky evening. The flamingos returned and, each tucking up a leg, burrowed their heads under their wings and settled down for the night. Gulls and terns settled companionably together. Elephant seals and sea lions took to the sea, calling out to one another. And most kids, most people, never had a chance to hear them, to spend a night alone on a beach. They missed a lot.

If Papa hadn't gone to the Martins' and had stayed

home, he'd just be finishing dinner. Grinding coffee. He'd miss their checker game. Maybe he'd run down and play chess with the doctor. More likely he'd stay home in case his son came back, and so he'd be trying to read. Worrying.

Maybe Papa didn't want Mama back. He didn't follow her to San Francisco before. He'd always said he wouldn't move away from Puerto Piramides, where his father and grandfathers had lived. Aside from going away to school he'd always lived here.

Mama's letter didn't sound all that eager or heartbroken, either. Samantha might say his mother wanted to be friends. And since she and Paolo were strangers, Mama thought Papa could help them get acquainted. That *was* what she wrote.

He kept thinking as he walked Pancho partway up the hill so the old horse could nibble grass before it got too dark. What would it be like—living with Mama, going to school with Samantha, migrating with the gray whales? Not that *he* wanted to, of course, but what was it Papa liked so much about going abroad to school?

Neither Samantha nor Luis would be around next year. He'd been miserably lonely the week he and Samantha weren't speaking. How would it be all year? But how could he live without Papa and their checker games and morning sketching safaris and . . . "You'll be back," Samantha had said, forgetting she'd run away for a week to teach her parents they couldn't just expect her to follow them to Puerto Piramides. A long shudder ran through him. The moon clearing the far hills seemed closer than San Francisco.

As darkness closed over the beach, each sound became distinct and a little frightening. He still heard in his mind the cry of that despairing sea lion pup. Saw the pup falling into a monstrous mouth filled with razor-sharp teeth. Unknown dangers lurked in the dark night.

Maybe a sea lion would lumber over and crush him while he slept. Accidentally, but crushed is crushed. How about wolves and coyotes? They traveled in packs. There wasn't much danger with the fire. But how could he keep up the fire if he fell asleep? Stop it! Papa always said this peninsula was a friendly place. And Pancho would hear an intruder and whinny, anyhow. *Then* he could worry.

As if to prove his point, a little later Pancho did whinny. Paolo heard rocks sliding down the path. *Something was coming!* He tried to peer into the darkness, but the fire blinded him and he could see nothing. Sliding rocks. Footsteps. Pancho whinnied again.

Suddenly a light flashed on. Someone had a lantern. A man. Paolo froze. His mouth felt dry, voiceless, but he had to know who it was. He had to ask!

"Who is it? What do you want?" His voice trembled, and he hated it for giving him away. Any robber would know he wasn't armed. And afraid. He looked around for driftwood to use as a club, but the woodpile was too far away. Out of reach. "Who is it?"

"Hello, down there! Paolo?"

"Papa, what are you doing here?" Unfortunately his father probably heard the relief in his voice.

"I've come for my game of checkers." And as Papa stepped into the light of the fire, he had not only a checkerboard but a sleeping bag under his arm.

SETTLING OLD SCORES

15 By the light of the fire Papa looked rumpled and tired, as if he'd slept in his clothes. And he smiled a little ruefully, as if he wasn't sure of his welcome—or why he'd come out on such a wild goose chase. Paolo wanted to jump up and give him a hug but remembered in time that he'd had good reason to leave this morning. "How did you find me?" he asked, with a grin he couldn't help.

"Elementary, my dear son. You brought me here once to draw penguins and said it was your favorite beach."

"But that was years ago. I'd forgotten."

"Well, yes, but it was an extraordinary choice for an eight-year-old, a beach without wet sand to build castles."

"I would have come home, Papa."

His father laid out his sleeping bag and sat down, setting checkers on the board, his head bent. When he looked up, lips pursed, his expression was thoughtful.

"Yes, I know, but I'd done such a damn fool thing

in giving you Leonora's letter without a word of explanation. I let you go off thinking that I'd stopped her coming, or refused her money, or kept her from writing letters. And it was inexcusable of me to assume that because I liked the idea of going away to school, you would too. I should know better."

Then Paolo, embarrassed, busied himself with putting wood on the fire. He should have known Papa wouldn't have refused Leonora money or letters. "Couldn't you have told me when she wrote? What did you and Mama fight about, aside from where we'd all live, when she came five years ago?"

"When she left, I did ask Leonora not to write me for a month or so, so I could catch my breath, and she's never let me forget it. As I remember, we didn't fight except about where we'd live. What's made it all so hard was that we still cared for each other."

" 'At least once before she's a mother of the groom—' " Paolo was shocked by the bitterness in his voice.

"Well, Leonora uses catch phrases to hide her own hurt. I read that one to mean she's regretted leaving you. Bitterly. That's why Señora Martin's invitation to live with them pained me. You'd rather live with Samantha—naturally—but it would break your mother's heart. She'd never say so, but I know."

"They only want me because they think I'm safe."

"Safe?"

"Not boyfriend material."

"Oh, Lord, Son."

Papa looked wistfully at the checkers. Just beyond the ring of firelight penguins circled round, curious, watching, red eyes gleaming in the dark. "Samantha hated coming to the peninsula, but she loves it here now and doesn't want to go home," Paolo murmured.

"I think you'll like San Francisco, Paolo, if you'll only give it a chance. But I didn't come to lecture you. Shall we play?"

"Samantha says I need a good education like yours to protect the animals here."

"She's right, Son. Red or black?"

"*Momentito*, Papa—about Mama. You sent a ticket and she didn't come?"

His father nodded, with a sigh, as he took his hand off the black checker he'd hoped to move. "I sent round-trip tickets twice and money for the divorce another time. She came once, five years ago. She never got the divorce."

"You mean you aren't divorced after thirteen years?"

"No. Argentina didn't have divorce then, and Leonora didn't get one in San Francisco. She knew I didn't care, and maybe she didn't want to marry again."

"That's not fair. And she wants you to visit—to try again?"

"Only to visit. To help you settle, I think. We're

both changed after all these years. And set in our ways. We'd be like strangers except for old problems. Here, I brought a few pictures."

Paolo heard both longing and finality in his father's voice. "So you won't move to San Francisco to be with her?"

"No, Son, never. I live in Puerto Piramides as my father and grandfathers did before me, and I hope you'll make this your home too. We're only talking of school. And I do feel guilty that I haven't helped you get to know your mother earlier, but I guess I wanted you to myself. I'm sorry."

Paolo nodded and took the small wooden box, inlaid with delicate enameled flowers on the lid. As he opened it the smell of cedar escaped, pungent in the night air. "Mama's box?"

"She left it with a note saying I had always been the keeper of our artifacts. You remind me of her— your sensitivity—the way your face lights up. She had to live in her own way, I suppose, but for both of us, you were worth everything, a joy." Papa looked into the fire.

Then why did she leave me? Why did she only come back once? But Papa's somber face kept him from asking. He examined the pictures carefully under the light of the lantern. There were about two dozen, Mama smiling, Mama laughing, Mama with a sad smile, several with his father and three of his mother and *Querido* Baby Gordo, as she wrote in that spidery hand, across the back. Was he like her? Did his face light up like hers when he was happy as Papa and Samantha said? What was she really like?

"I always think of her as she was when she visited, but here she looks so young, hardly older than Samantha."

"She was in college," said Papa, a little stiffly.

"She seems older, more serious in these two pictures with you, Papa." Unhappy, maybe? Luis said how he'd feel depended on what his father was like. Just because she and Papa didn't want the same kind of life didn't necessarily mean he and Mama wouldn't see eye to eye. "I always thought of her coming back, never of going to see Mama and her life."

"You might be pleasantly surprised," Papa said.

Paolo went through the photos again and again, trying to make up a person of the pictures, to imprint each photo on his brain. Then he closed the box and handed it back to his father. "She reminds me of Samantha. How did you meet?"

"They're yours. I should have given them to you before. How did we meet? Oh, my. One of my students introduced us, and we married three weeks later."

"Three weeks later!" But his father was staring into the fire with the saddest expression. "Thank you, Papa. You keep the photos. I'll borrow them sometimes. Let me keep this one where she's smiling. She isn't coming again?"

His father shook his head.

"And so you want me to go to her instead?"

"Yes, to know your mother and for your education. I'm not going to kidnap you, Paolo, or throw you out of the house, but I would like you to try one year. Then, if you don't like it, we'll do something else—but leave the bay and swim in the ocean, like White Calf must."

"But if Luis could stay in school?" Paolo reached for his father's hand. The older man took it in both of his. Paolo felt the love between them, but he still couldn't quite make himself say he'd leave.

"Luis works and nurses his mama, two big jobs."

Paolo sighed. "White Calf. Luis wanted to go out this morning. He said he had to make peace and see the albino and his mother again—but I said it was too soon."

"Foolhardy! Mothers remember. But I know how he feels. You and I might go out and see if we can find White Calf. Find out if his mother holds Luis against us."

"Tomorrow?"

His father nodded. "And now, Paolo, could we please play checkers and turn in while there are stars in the sky?"

Paolo heard the finality in his tone. This conversation was over. Okay. He'd ask more questions tomorrow. Let it all go until tomorrow. He chose the reds and they commenced to play.

After Papa won two games he climbed into his

sleeping bag. In a very few minutes his gentle snoring fell into place with the other night sounds—with the yelping of the seals, the barking penguins, and the hooting owls.

But Paolo was too stirred up to sleep. He lay awake a long while, going over and over the conversation with Papa, passing Mama's photos before his mind's eye, one by one, the story of his life, too. Did she still think of him as Baby Gordo? How old was she now? What was she like? Was it possible they could love each other as he and Papa did?

She only came for a few days that one visit. About all he remembered, aside from the arguments with Papa, was a walk he and Mama had taken. He'd loved hearing her laughter, light and understanding somehow. But she kept asking what he thought and then listening so hard it made him shy and he answered in whispers. Finally Mama had said, "Gordito, you're as closemouthed as your papa." He'd been proud at the time, and he laughed aloud now at how frustrated she must have been. Poor Mama.

Dear Mama—he began the letter he would write— *I am lying here on the beach trying to remember everything about you.* What should he say next? But lulled by the bark of the seals and roll of the sea, he drifted off to sleep. Tomorrow. He could think about it all tomorrow.

WHALES IN THE MORNING

16 It was late when they reached their boat because Paolo had had to take Pancho home first and pick up their wet suits. The sun was aleady clearing the horizon, but the beach still felt cool and fresh and untouched. He and Papa were shy after last night, a little uncertain what they'd agreed and what was all right to talk about. However, Paolo felt that something between them, some wall, was crumbling. Papa had said he wouldn't make him go to San Francisco. And he could always come back. He had choices. It would be his decision.

They smiled at each other, untied the boat, and hauled it over the sand and through the breakers without comment, working smoothly as was their habit.

"In you go," Papa said, hoisting himself over the side.

"Good." Was it only the day before yesterday he'd come out here with Luis and Samantha? Better not bring *that* up.

Papa started the motor and settled back. He's happy, Paolo thought. They were watching the gulls that trailed in the boat's wake, in the hope of handouts. Seals and dolphins played in the sun-dappled water around them. Papa pointed out two whale blows and headed toward them.

He cut the motor as they drew close to three whales lying quietly at the surface, the sun shining purple on their gray hides. One blew, an eerie whistling sound, and the other two turned and dove slowly, coming around and drifting beneath them, gigantic shadows passing without so much as rocking the boat. Then, surfacing a few yards away, the whales faced the boat, as if to say, your turn.

Paolo braced himself for the safety lecture that always came before he and Papa could even think of swimming.

"Playing with us." Papa grinned, throwing over the anchor and watching as it dropped, disappearing into the deep green sea. "Let's give them a few minutes before our swim. Nervous after your adventure the other day?"

Paolo shook his head, smiling, still waiting.

"Don't see your special friends this morning."

"Luis spooked them or they've left the bay."

"Maybe, maybe not. It's a good-sized bay."

These whales were sunning themselves, two full grown and one calf, three purple-gray mounds in the bay.

"Ready?" Papa asked.

"I'll follow you." No advice. That was a change!

Paolo missed White Calf. Maybe they'd left the bay and he'd never see them again. Maybe his mother just needed time to forget Luis's pushiness. Were they still friends?

He took off his shirt and slipped over the side of the boat and into the cold sea. He and his father swam quietly around the boat, giving the whales time to grow accustomed to their presence. He was at home in the water in a new way since he'd hauled Luis back to the boat. As light and easy as a dolphin. Almost.

One of the whales grew curious, moving closer in. He and Papa swam alongside this whale, maybe sixty feet long, its gray hide encrusted with barnacles, old scars, and sea worms. It was like the hull of a ship, a towering living ship. The whale's alert eyes seemed to consider them, and she held still while they completed their inspection.

"Friendly," Paolo murmured as they surfaced.

"We're her guests," Papa replied, swimming by. Paolo watched his father's paddling feet, slow and easy, and followed in his wake.

Then Papa backed off a few yards and dove, not trying to go under the whale but deep enough to examine the hide underwater. After a moment, Paolo followed. A school of smelt, iridescent silver, flashed around him and streaked on.

The whale shifted and the churning water sent Paolo swimming toward the boat.

Papa reached out and caught his shoulder, stopping him. "Here comes the calf. Maybe we can watch her nurse."

Paolo saw the calf come alongside its mother, red callosities shimmering on its sleek young hide. In a few minutes, after the water calmed, they figured they wouldn't startle the whales. Papa and Paolo followed. They swam underwater and watched the calf nose around the soft place on her mother's belly, before they had to come up for air.

"Next year we'll bring scuba gear," Papa said.

"Yes! Imagine staying down for half an hour." Paolo treasured the surge of pleasure the sight of the mother and the calf had given him.

"Pretty miraculous, isn't it?" Papa asked.

Paolo nodded, putting his answer into his smile.

When he'd gotten his wind, Paolo dove again and caught a glimpse of the calf nursing under the mother, drifting in her comforting shadow, only a few inches below her. Just a glimpse and then he had to surface for air, but it was enough. "Miraculous."

"Ready to go?" Papa asked.

It was enough. Paolo nodded and hoisted himself into the boat. He hauled up the anchor while his father started the motor. They smiled at each other.

"I'll never forget this morning if I live to be a hundred. Oh, thank you, Papa." The words burst from Paolo only later, when they were beaching the skiff.

"I've seen a calf nursing just once before. I was about your age. Made me a naturalist, Son," Papa replied.

"About the age you went away to school, too, wasn't it?" Paolo asked quietly.

"Yes, to Boston." Papa nodded, suddenly intent on the work of securing the lines of the skiff.

EVERYTHING CHANGES

17 "Luis had to work, but I would have gone out to hunt for you if you hadn't come home," Samantha said late the following afternoon. They were sitting on Paolo's favorite broad flat rock behind the Hotel Tourista, watching for White Calf while they waited for Señora Martin to finish correcting tests and lock up the school.

Paolo stared out at the bay, hunting for White Calf. The wind was scattering clouds across the sky that reflected in shadows hopscotching over the water, making it hard to spot either whales or their blows.

"Oh, I knew you were okay, but I thought you might want a friend," Samantha continued, standing up and peering out over the bay with her binoculars, but after a moment she sat down again, her hair brushing Paolo's shoulder.

"Yes. I kept thinking what you'd say and what I'd say." His heart raced, but he wasn't about to tell her how much he'd wished she were there.

"And what did you want me to say?"

"The whole town knows I cut school on Friday.

Papa told everyone he'd run away with his son." Paolo rested his hand on Samantha's, ignoring her question.

"Boasting. All the men are a little *macho,* even your papa," Samantha said, taking his hand.

"Pride?"

"In case you haven't noticed, he's proud of anything you do," said Samantha with a toss of her blond head. Then in a softer voice, "Gordo, are you really so miserable? About going, about me, oh, you know—everything."

"You know how I feel about you. I've never known any girl—ever—I mean, maybe I do need someone to help me across the street, after all."

"Then you're coming with us?"

Paolo felt the letter he'd written to Mama in his shirt pocket. He'd told Papa he would go—to know Mama—but he hadn't told Samantha yet. He wasn't ready—she took too much for granted. "We have a street in Puerto Piramides, too," he said.

Samantha whispered something before she suddenly withdrew her hand and stood up. She'd whispered something, but he couldn't hear what because Luis came running up, out of breath and pointing to the bay. Five whales were lined up like submarines, one after another, heading for open sea, awesome as their seasonal instinct told them to move on.

"There they go. There goes White Calf. There goes my job taking tourists whale watching," said Luis.

"There they go, the last of the dinosaurs," Samantha added as she passed her binoculars to Paolo.

"I think I see him," Paolo said, focusing.

White Calf surfaced, jumping high, visibly white, before he flipped back and hit the water with a splash of foam. He submerged and reappeared, apparently playing with another calf. The two calves swam up under a clump of seaweed and White Calf rolled over, scooping seaweed with his flippers.

"Your friend's playing jump rope," Samantha said, taking back the binoculars.

"Think he'll still be lighter than the others when he comes back next year? Will I recognize him?"

"Maybe his mother will forget me by next year," Luis said. "White Calf liked me."

Paolo nodded. He couldn't speak. He choked up every year, watching the whales leave. And this year, watching White Calf go and knowing he might never recognize him again, was like losing someone in his family! Saturday, out with Papa, he'd sensed the whales were resting up to leave.

Seabirds skimmed the water, riding wind currents, following the whales as one after another answered the mysterious call. Migration. A ceremony of days. How could whales know when their calves were ready for the open sea? Paolo felt as if part of him swam out to sea with them and he wouldn't be whole again until he stood on this cliff next summer and watched them come home.

"What are you thinking, Paolo? Tell me," demanded Samantha.

He grinned. Then suddenly he stood up and called to White Calf. *"Mnnnnnnh, ah-uuuuuomm, oooooohhhmmm."* He took off his cap and waved it high over his head.

"He'll hear you," Luis said.

"But will I be here when he comes back?" Paolo asked, calling again and again until his throat ached with strain.

Suddenly a strange high hum seemed to float over the water, just once, leaving Paolo wondering if he'd really heard a whale call or only the wind. He grabbed Luis by the arm. "Did you hear something?"

"White Calf was saying *hasta luego*—until we meet again." Luis's voice was low and sad.

"Even the whales answer you," Samantha added. "I'll never forget this as long as I live."

"Hasta luego," Paolo murmured, overcome by the longing that shook him, the happiness that flooded his body. He felt weak in the knees and had to sit down. White Calf had answered! At least, one whale had called.

"Where will you be? You're going, then?" Luis frowned, standing over him. "Your mama's taking you in, after all?"

He's mad at me for leaving him, Paolo thought, his mind still on the miracle of White Calf's call. He shrugged and changed the subject. "What'll you do when the tourists go?"

"Maybe work on the fishing boats—Señora Martin told the foreman I'm sixteen. She says it's only a white lie and I can pass, no?" Luis stood up tall, his eyes worried.

"You can pass for sixteen, easy," Paolo said.

"Good money and home by noon. Six days a week. The only thing is I can't help Mama in the morning."

"There's a hospital in Puerto Madryn."

"She won't go—doesn't want to die among strangers."

Samantha reached out and took Luis's hand. Paolo turned away, back toward the whales. But he saw only one; the others must have cleared the bay.

Then the two calves surfaced again, White Calf and his friend, trailing streamers of seaweed, breaching with a tremendous splash, diving, surfacing again. Playing. Putting off leaving as long as possible. Like him.

Paolo handed the binoculars to Luis. "Your turn. They're playing like we used to," he said gently.

Luis watched a long while. Finally he lowered the binoculars and turned back to the others. "They're gone. Yes, friends like us, Gordo. And for them also, everything is changing."

"In two weeks we graduate," Samantha said.

"Then Christmas and the New Year," Paolo added mournfully.

"Then you go away together and I'm alone."

"Nursing your mama, working the boats. Two full-time jobs, Papa says." Paolo felt tongue-tied, as if none of them were saying all that was in their hearts, how they hated parting. Why couldn't he say *he* admired Luis?

"Your papa said that?" Luis's smile was easy, proud.

"We all think you're a good son, but you get so insulted if anyone says anything nice about you that we keep our traps shut," Samantha said, giving Luis a hug.

"I can go by and check on your mama mornings while you're out fishing," Paolo added.

"Me too. She likes my American accent when I read to her."

"Until you leave." Luis seemed to be considering.

Paolo wanted to shout. He wouldn't leave. For a crazy moment the sick woman seemed a reason to stay, though he'd never gotten along with her and couldn't help much. He nodded.

"The boy who loves whales," Luis said, turning then and facing them. There were tears in his eyes.

Paolo watched to see if Luis was putting him down, but he saw only tenderness in his friend's face.

"They'll come back. And you'd better, Gordo!"

"I haven't said I'm even leaving yet."

Luis merely raised an eyebrow. "Good friends. Could you give Mama her breakfast? Until I find someone?"

"Of course," said Paolo.

"Thanks. Well, the whales have gone. I'm late. *Hasta*," he said, and took off at a run.

They watched him run down the hill, tunneling dust in his wake, cross the road, and then disappear into the small adobe house where his mother lay waiting.

"He's actually letting us help. Unbelievable! That's a big step for Luis," Samantha said softly. Then, more briskly, "We'll set up a schedule."

"Imagine hearing your mother talking about dying."

"Oh, Gordo, shut up! Unless you want me to start crying. How can I leave him all alone?"

"Maybe Mama will let us phone him." There, he'd told her he was going. And she was so upset, she hadn't noticed.

Samantha was quiet a long while, and then she smiled. "Next year you'll see two migrations—in the winter the gray whales go south, right past San Francisco, and then you'll be back here in time to welcome White Calf—any naturalist's dream."

Paolo nodded, suddenly too choked up to speak. He'd forgotten about the gray whales.

They looked out to sea once more, scanning the horizon, but there were no whale tracks. White Calf was gone. "Let's go," Paolo said huskily.

Papa would be waiting. He should walk Samantha down to the school and go on home.

But he didn't move. Graduation. Then everything

would change. Forever. No matter what, there was no way he could keep everyone with him as they were today and this was what he wanted, wanted more than anything in the whole world. Might as well mail the letter to Mama.

Samantha was beautiful as she stood, hands on hips, the sun setting behind her. She turned and grinned at him.

He grinned back as the *toot-toot* of a familiar horn sounded. Señora Martin and Charley were in the Jeep on the road below, honking for Samantha, heading back to Whale Camp.

"Hurry it up, baby. Charley is giving me a beastly headache," Señora Martin called.

"You're not my mother!" Charley screamed.

"Uh-oh, Spoonheart again," Samantha said, frowning.

Paolo reached for her hand and held on. "Let's go," he said, and they ran down the hill together, swinging their hands, suddenly laughing, pushed by a balmy wind.

"Paolo, you've got to make them stop. They want to give Spoonheart back to his herd. And he's mine!"

"Baby, he wants to go back. He showed you that," Señora Martin explained in a weary voice.

"Spoonheart jumped through the living room window to follow another guanaco yesterday," Samantha explained.

"Next time he'll cut his throat. Will you help us take

him back to the wild, Paolo? He wants his herd and we can't take him home, anyhow. Charley, you can visit him. Please calm down, dear. You know it's best."

"I do not!"

"Mama says you can have a dog the day we get home."

"I want to live with Spoonheart the rest of my life. No dog can compare with him. I like him better than all of you put together."

"Oh, I do hope not."

"Especially you! You are not my mother."

"Sounds good to me," said Señora Martin, opening the back door and motioning Samantha in.

"If you loved me, we'd keep Spoonheart."

"I might have considered more carefully if I'd known you were a package deal. Paolo, dear, could you help? Your papa is coming. Tomorrow?"

"I guess so." Maybe Papa would give her the sketch of baby Spoonheart to take home.

"Traitor!" Charley screamed back at him as the Jeep pulled away in a cloud of dust.

18 At dawn the following morning Paolo and his father stopped the Jeep near the meadow where Samantha first saw Spoonheart five months ago. A season of whales and guanacos. They'd agreed to meet the Martins here at six and then, if the herd didn't appear, they'd all scout them. Early morning when a herd started grazing offered the best chance of finding them together.

"Plenty of hoofprints. Too bad we can't see over the rise, but it's better not to risk spooking the guanacos," Papa said.

"Both Spoonheart and Charley are probably being impossible. She called me a traitor yesterday." Paolo laughed uneasily.

"Aren't you thinking more of the guanaco than her?"

"Can you imagine Spoonheart in their house in San Francisco?"

"She's only six years old, Son."

"But Luis brought the guanaco, not me. Why am I a traitor?"

"Because Spoonheart and Charley trust you."

"Trusted."

They'd parked near a meadow of pampa grass and spiny bushes, favorite guanaco food. The wind blowing off the water smelled sweetly of sage and of the sea. If only they'd see some larks. Papa particularly wanted to sketch meadowlarks for an article nearing deadline and he'd brought a sketchbook and pencils, just in case.

"While we're waiting, could you try a lark call?"

Paolo whistled the three-toned trill of the lark.

After a pause they heard a reply.

Paolo called again. Another reply. "There, Papa, the grass by the red cactus."

"Ah, bless you, Son—a fine pair." He drew out his colored pencils and pad and set to work. Paolo watched as the birds skittered about in the grass, fascinated at how Papa caught their soft beige color, the yellow shading, and the bobbing topknot. In ten minutes he'd finished, stuffing pens back in a windbreaker pocket and the pad into a string shoulder bag. "That's a relief."

"Papa, I mailed the letter to Mama yesterday."

"Good. I almost stuffed your shirt in the washing machine and spotted that envelope in the pocket just in time. So?"

"Like I told you, I'll go for one school year. If she still wants me."

"I'm proud of you, Paolo."

They trudged through the grass in silence. There was too much to say, and Paolo knew that neither he nor Papa had any idea how to start. When he saw a family of tuco-tuco rats, Paolo pointed, but Papa shook his head.

Then they saw a half-grown ostrich standing in tall grass, and Papa took out his pad and started to draw again. The ostrich stood, alert to danger, poised for flight, but hesitating. Paolo didn't know how, but Papa caught this tension in his sketch. He looked up and smiled. Pleased.

"Lucky the Martins are late," he whispered. "And by the way, Paolo, try to imagine living here if animals and birds didn't interest you. They do not interest Leonora. She said the silence was driving her crazy, and I hadn't the faintest idea what she meant—with the birds and the wind and the sea it never seemed silent to me."

"I can't imagine not being interested." In his own way Papa was trying to tell him something and without his asking! Maybe because of the letter. And then, surprising himself, he threw his arms around Papa and hugged him.

His father smiled and nodded. "Thanks, Son. I needed that. I'm going to miss you badly. Oh, here come the Martins."

Dr. Martin brought the red Jeep in next to theirs and cut the engine. Then Charley slammed open the car door and bounced out after the guanaco, her ponytail bobbing. "Spoonheart, come back here!"

"Where is he?" Paolo asked, coming up to her. The guanaco was on the other side of the car, sniffing the air, straining at the expandable leash Charley had snapped to a dog collar around his neck.

"If you've come for Spoonheart, you can just get back in your car. Paolo, you're the worst traitor in the world."

"Charley, he needs to go."

"How about me?"

"You have a family. Let Spoonheart have one too."

"No, he's in our family. He's mine."

"He's a wild animal and you've been his friend."

"That's a rare trust, Charley," Papa added gently, and then followed Señora and Dr. Martin and Samantha, who were walking toward the rise to see if the herd was nearby.

Charley stopped then, bewildered, her little face all freckles and frightened blue eyes under curly red hair. She focused on Paolo, stared at him a long moment, and then burst into tears. She plopped down on the sand, sobbing hard. The guanaco peered around the Jeep tentatively.

Paolo sat down too and put his arms around Charley. "You've been a good friend to him. He couldn't have lived without you giving him milk, blankets, his first food, saving him from poachers."

"I did, didn't I?" Charley asked between sobs.

"Getting up in the middle of the night for feedings."

"Mama said she'd nursed enough babies," Charley added, sniffling.

Paolo nodded, watching the guanaco edging slowly toward them.

"Then—why—doesn't Spoonheart—liiiiike me?"

"What makes you think he doesn't like you?" He'd seen the guanaco butt and spit, but Charley was a funny kid. She might be thinking of something else entirely.

"He never waits for me to come home from school."

"He's not a dog, he's a wild animal. He likes you."

And, as if to prove Paolo right, the guanaco sidled up to Charley as she sat crying and rubbed against her so hard she toppled over.

"Oooh, Spoonheart. You did come back."

A high bleat answered her.

"But if you leave, I won't have anyone for me." Charley looked up at the furry young male, and Spoonheart lowered his head and allowed himself to be petted.

"He'll be using the guanaco communal dung heap soon."

"Oh, yeah? He's used to our smells, not theirs. He'll probably get constipated and it'll be your fault."

Paolo decided to let that one pass, though he couldn't help grinning. "You feel like I do about White Calf leaving."

"But you can't hug a whale and I can hug Spoon-heart—sometimes."

"But I love him, and I watched him leave yesterday."

Charley dried her eyes and stood up. "Poor Paolo! Can I visit Spoonheart at least?"

"I think we can find him again. A fox I fed went back to the wild and he'd come sometimes if I called him." Paolo held out his hand. Charley took it and climbed to her feet. Hand in hand they started walking toward the rise.

"Have any trouble getting Spoonheart in the car?"

"Spoonheart loooves to ride in cars. We've taken him along on drives before so he just hopped in back with me and Samantha and sat there, looking out like any tourist."

Señora Martin held her finger to her lips, cautioning them to be quiet as they neared the top of the hill where the others waited. Spoonheart had run ahead and was straining at his leash, pulling Charley with him. He kept sniffing the air. Reluctantly Charley took off his collar.

On gaining the rise, Spoonheart stopped still, ears forward, immobile. Paolo ran up and, standing next to the guanaco, looked down into the meadow. The herd was there, all right. Fifty or more guanacos and several ostriches were grazing in the brush where Samantha had found Spoonheart. Spoonheart shivered, looked over at Charley, shivered again.

"He'll go. He's just thinking," Charley said gloomily.

"He *has* to," whispered Samantha.

"We've time. Let him get used to the idea," said Papa.

"I know just how he feels," said Paolo.

"Good. Then watch closely, Son."

Spoonheart bleated tentatively.

Several of the guanacos answered, but still Spoonheart stood as if rooted to the ground.

"Maybe he's shy," Samantha said. "What were you two talking about?"

"Saying good-bye," Paolo whispered, his shoulder touching Samantha's.

Her blue eyes considered him, as her little sister's had.

Spoonheart took a few steps toward the herd but stopped short of starting down the hill.

"Should we go and leave him to get acquainted, Charley?" asked Dr. Martin.

"Oh, please, Daddy, not yet. Maybe they won't like him. Maybe he doesn't want to go back. Stay a bit!"

Paolo heard the desperation in Charley's voice, and Samantha reached over and took her sister's hand. They watched in silence as Spoonheart gingerly started picking his way through the brush on the hillside. When he reached the meadow, he turned and let out a long, high-pitched bleat before he turned back and walked steadily into the herd.

"He's saying good-bye," Charley said.

"And maybe thank you," added Samantha.

Charley gave her sister a grateful look.

The guanacos in the herd appeared to take no particular notice. From time to time one of them would look over at the newcomer, as if considering. Slowly Spoonheart dropped his head and began nibbling at the coarse grass. After a few minutes he looked up, alert, ears tensed. He looked straight at them and then around at the grazing herd and dropped his head again.

"We can go now," Charley said, walking toward the car without a backward glance.

19 Two weeks later Paolo picked up a letter from Mama at the post office. The answer to his letter. He shoved the envelope unopened in his shirt pocket, zipped in so it wouldn't get lost.

"I've felt the same way about opening Leonora's letters, but what can she say, after all? You haven't asked for money," Papa said, sorting through the rest of the mail for checks or personal letters.

If she said he couldn't stay with her, that would suit him fine. Wouldn't it? But he'd written more than he'd intended about remembering her and opening this letter meant reading what she had to say back. Could be embarrassing. He'd open it later.

That afternoon Paolo stood in the sun, waiting while Señora Martin and her daughters locked up the school. He'd made the mistake of telling Charley he thought he'd seen Spoonheart running with his herd and, of course, Charley wanted to visit him.

"Charley's foaming at the mouth because Mom's slow," Samantha said, coming up beside him.

"Did she like Papa's sketch of Spoonheart?" Paolo asked, thinking that between the sun on her hair and her smile Samantha was incredibly beautiful.

"It's on the wall at the foot of her bed so it's the last thing she sees at night and the first in the morning."

"All I hope is, if we find Spoonheart, that he remembers who fed him and cleaned up after him," added Señora Martin, locking the door.

"Can you really call him in, Gordo?" asked Charley, stuffing lettuce and carrots into a plastic bag.

"He didn't come to me yesterday, but he trotted to the edge of the herd and bleated. I hope they're still there."

"Gordo can call in *any* animal," Samantha said.

"Well, climb in and let's go see, kids," said Señora Martin, turning the key in the Jeep's ignition.

"If he spits at me, at least it means he remembers me," said Charley as they neared the meadow where Paolo had seen the guanacos the day before.

The herd was across the road and grazing new grass under outcroppings of sagebrush. They stopped and quietly got out of the car. Samantha handed Charley the binoculars, and her mother helped her adjust them.

"They all look alike," Charley whispered.

Paolo nodded. He gave his best imitation of the

curious high whinny of a lead guanaco. Several animals pricked up their ears, but none moved. They waited several minutes.

"You try calling, Charley," he whispered.

Charley whistled as she had at home. Then she called gently, "Spoonheart, Spoonheart."

A young male looked up and, ever so slowly, moved to their edge of the herd, ears straight up. At the edge of the herd the guanaco stopped, as if considering.

"Oh, Spoonheart, lettuce and carrots! Spoonheart, please," Charley crooned.

And then Spoonheart lifted his head and trotted away from the herd, picking up speed as he neared them and saw the lettuce and carrots Charley held. He sprinted across the road and almost knocked Charley over in his eagerness.

"Oh, Spoonheart! Oh, Spoonheart, you do remember," Charley said over and over as she fed the animal, timidly touching, and finally petting him. Spoonheart didn't much like to be touched as he ate and had been known to give her a nasty buck with his head. However, today as he finished the lettuce and carrots, treats from his domesticated days, he nuzzled Charley quite gently.

"Oh, honey, if you could only tell me what it's like. Are you happy, Spoonheart?" Charley asked, hugging him.

But once the food was gone, the guanaco grew restive, showing no interest in Señora Martin, or Samantha, or even Paolo, his old favorite. With a last nuzzle for Charley, he loped across the road and back to his herd. In a very few minutes it wasn't possible to distinguish him from half a dozen other young males cropping grass under the sage.

"Time to go, kids," said Señora Martin. "Happy, baby?"

"Finally, we're friends," Charley said with a sigh, climbing into the backseat of the red Jeep.

"He didn't even look at the rest of us," Paolo said.

"Yes, I know. Spoonheart only loves me," Charley replied.

"I feel like I've seen a miracle," said Samantha, tears running down her cheeks.

"Oh, stop it, Samantha. If anyone has a right to cry it's me, and I'm not."

But Samantha laid her head on Paolo's shoulder and went right on crying, and he gently put an arm around her. "You know that I'm an awful crybaby," she whispered.

"That's okay, Samantha. That's just fine," he replied.

The house was quiet when Paolo returned. Papa hadn't yet come in. He flopped on the couch, in sole possession of his home, the room reflecting a soft yellow-pink haze from the sunset. The wind had dropped, and he could hear surf lapping the beach.

He'd been moved by Spoonheart's nuzzling Charley and he still felt Samantha's imprint, felt her lying quietly in his arms as she cried, as if she belonged there. He lay on the couch, letting it all sink in.

And finally in the gathering twilight he took out Mama's letter, badly crumpled but still smelling faintly of lavender, and read.

Dearest Paolo,

You can't imagine how I'm looking forward to having you here, getting to know you, my own beloved son coming from his home in Patagonia. All the possibilities! Your letter dazzles me. Like sunlight. I didn't dream you'd thought so much about us.

I always felt I knew you rather well that one year and, in some sense, we must be pretty well ourselves by the time we've been in this world a full year, don't you suppose?

Or so I've comforted myself all these days and years without you. Every once in a while I take a notion to soar down and scoop you up, but it dissipates. Partly cowardice, but I also know Raul is a born father and can imagine you two stalking the birds rising from dawn nests, preparing dinner together, playing chess. Oh, dear, if only he didn't always have to win. Perhaps he's mellowed?

Shall we become friends, then? Though it is true you have a flighty mother, I will answer letters honestly. And then, when we do meet, I hope we won't stop talking for a month and a half because of all the intriguing thoughts we've

begun on paper. Committed to paper? What do
you say, Paolo? Shall we begin?

Your loving Mama

He was still lying on the couch, the letter in one
hand, tears drying on his cheeks, when his father came
in. He handed him the letter.

With a sigh, Papa sat on the whale disk and read.
"A magic lady," he said when he'd finished.

"And you were married three weeks after you met?"
Papa nodded. "Of course."

"Maybe *she'll* come back."

"I don't think so, Son." Then, after a long silence,
"Leonora knows it would still be a barren life for her.
At least she gives me credit for mellowing."

His father's grin was wistful, and he went into the
kitchen and began taking food out of the refrigerator
for dinner. It was his turn to cook. "Spaghetti or
steak?"

"Spaghetti, please."

"I was afraid of that." Papa started chopping onions.
"So what do we do now?"

The question hung in the air. Paolo paced the floor
silently, the only sound the steady rhythm of his father
chopping onions, then green pepper, then parsley,
then mushrooms. He loved to hear Papa chopping
vegetables. "Will you come up with me?" he asked
finally.

"Depends on what it costs. Señora Martin can brief

your new school principal on our curriculum better than I can. I suppose I should see my American publisher. And Mama. But only for a week or so. Coming home to an empty house will be pretty grim, though."

"I'll write every week, and I'll be home when the whales return." Paolo grinned. "Hey, I'm feeling sorry for you, Papa."

"About time. I'll miss you, Son. But you'll come in June. For the North American summer. You'll beat the whales home."

Paolo wanted to say more, so much more, but it was hard to know how to begin. So he tried to imagine getting up every morning in San Francisco, Mama's apartment, a big city school. "Say, Papa, what do you know about gray whales?"

Graduation morning Paolo was just waking when he heard someone pounding on the door. He stumbled to his feet, glanced at his father's note—he'd gone walking alone so the graduate could sleep—and groped his way to the door.

"Coming. Coming. Hold your horses."

It was Samantha, shoving an enormous package wrapped in butcher paper with pictures all over it into his arms. "Happy graduation! Charley stayed up half the night doing the pictures, so she says you had better appreciate them."

"What are you doing here so early?" he asked, trying to keep his eyes open.

"What you should say is—'Thank you for the fabulous present,' " Samantha replied. "Luis and Mom and I have been over at the school decorating for an hour. Get some clothes on and come help—after you open your present, that is."

Fortunately Papa had signed two copies of his book, one for Luis and one for Samantha, and Paolo had been collecting specimen shells for her and they'd put them all in a turtle shell last night.

Still, for sheer bulk alone, her gift was momentous. Soft. He poked. Soft.

"Open iiiiiit!"

"Let me brush my teeth first."

"Three minutes, no more."

In what seemed less than three minutes he returned, dressed and carrying scissors.

When it was open, he couldn't believe his eyes. "But Samantha, your diary quilt, the one you were making to show your class—your snapshot quilt! For me?"

"I've been making it for you, lately anyhow. So you'll take your home away to school with you. See, that's you with the bandaged head. And there's Spoonheart. And the whales coming—and going. Penguins. My best squares."

"And here's White Calf! Samantha!" He was dumbfounded. "Samantha, this is the most wonderful present I've ever had in my whole life." She looked up from the quilt, and Paolo took her face in his hands to kiss her on both cheeks in the Argentine fashion but somehow—later he was never sure what happened—he kissed her lips instead.

After a moment, she gently pushed him away. "Next year," she said. "Promise me, next year?"

"Next year in San Francisco," Paolo said.

GLOSSARY

amigo: friend
Basta!: Enough!
Bueno: good, all right
Buenos días: Good morning
café con leche: coffee with milk
Caramba: Darn it
casita: little house
chulengo: baby guanaco
criollo horse: Argentine horse
difícil: hard
estancias: ranches
Estúpido!: Stupid!
flan: custard pudding
Gracias: Thanks
guanaco: an animal belonging to the same family as
   a llama
hasta: until
Hasta luego: Until we meet again
hijo: son, boy
Hola!: Hello!
jóvenes: young people

locos: crazy ones
macho: a very strong sense of male pride
magnífico: grand
malo: bad, naughty
maravilla: a wonder
médico: doctor
momentito: right away, one moment
nada: nothing
norte: north
polenta: stew with cornmeal
por favor: please
puchero: lamb stew
Qué pasa?: What's going on?
Querida: a term of endearment, darling
Rápido!: Hurry up!
Salvarme: Save me
Señora: Mrs.
simpático: congenial
Vamos!: Let's go!
viejo: old man